Hunger the Night

Stray Cat's Philosophy

DAVID PAUL MITCHELL

authorHOUSE

AuthorHouse™
1663 Liberty Drive
Bloomington, IN 47403
www.authorhouse.com
Phone: 833-262-8899

Published by AuthorHouse 04/09/2025

ISBN: 979-8-8230-4493-6 (sc)
ISBN: 979-8-8230-4492-9 (e)

Library of Congress Control Number: 2025904709

Print information available on the last page.

Those that hunger with a passion will find a familiarity with this tale. When it touches you, it's like the sensation felt before, and so remember, that the power is still in you. Hunger the Night.

Prologue

"LOOK WHAT WE'VE CREATED, AT our handiwork! We will change the world forever." Max went to the console, and activated the steel curtain which hid what was behind the shatterproof glass wall.

His genetic engineers looked upon their creation; years of reading genetic code, and gene splicing, changing, and manipulating the very blueprints of life. They had tampered with the chromosomes in a living organism, and won. Max's companies had mastered the plans for life, and were successful in manufacturing a new species. The team had designed something extraordinary.

Max was a multi-billionaire from the inheritance of his father's estate, but his true desire was to make his own unique waves in the world's economic structure. The media never gave full credit for his genius, and that motivated Max to go beyond conventional boundaries to get recognition.

Julie hesitantly uttered, "Right..., but it doesn't look like a domestic cow. She looks like a monster from one of my nightmares, and a thousand times more dangerous!"

Max retorted, "But it's exactly what the world will need in less than ten years my dear, and we did it first, rejoice! This cow is our future, the world needs this hybrid creature, and I did it first!"

Living it, and loving it; those words were Maxwell's key phrase when hard-pressed goals were accomplished, and everyone who knew him associated those words as his checkered flag for victory.

Max addressed his crew, "In less than ten years famine will make way into the First World. Third world populations are out of control, and putting critical strains on the First World nations to supply food. In ten years the First World won't be able to provide enough livestock to feed the rest of the world, unless something radical is done. Guess what? I did it!"

Max gambled his fortune on what these renegade scientists promised they could do if they had the financial backing. They wanted to break the DNA code, and re-write it. Max was going to put his name all over their accomplishments.

Breaking the code was one matter, but using it in a most profitable way was where his kind of genius was applied. Max was a futurist, but he didn't want to produce an army of genetically altered humans without souls to take over the planet for a radical dictator, and he wasn't going to create comic book-like humans to roam the skies as superheroes. Nope, Maxwell's grand plan was to corner the market with his patent on genetically altered livestock, and save the world from hunger.

Poor people were accustomed to hunger in the night, going to sleep on an empty stomach with a digestive system growling like a wild animal in want of a solid meal, but people who could afford meat, and poultry would pay any amount to avoid that uncomfortable feeling every night. Max had positioned his companies to reap that eventuality.

Futurist proclaimed that the world's oceans with its endless bounty of fish would solve the world's hunger problems, but how so when industrialization was polluting the spawning beds, and the world's great fishing fleets plundered the oceans without pause.

Beef, ham, and poultry were domesticated animals basically created by Man through selective breeding to get hybrid specimens for consumption, none of which would survive in their present forms in nature. Max actually had gone far beyond that level by rewriting the chromosome code of these domestics with direct genetic manipulation. Behind the glass wall was a so-called cow with the girth of an African hippopotamus. In fact it was part hippo. The geneticist had written hippo code into the domestic's genes to increase its meat ratio five times beyond a cow's yield in consumables. Unfortunately the hippo's nasty temperament was carried through to the end product.

"But Max, she's very unstable; it may be more hippo than cow. The FDA will never okay it as livestock, plus it doesn't look like a cow."

Max countered, "Aesthetics is not my concern, the public will never see it, only eat it, as long as it tastes like beef then we can sell it, and we've passed that test. We're getting five cow's worth of meat at a fraction of the cost of feeding three cows, and that's a profit in any rancher's book."

"But Max, she's injured members of my team, and Ben is dead. We need more time to delete its super aggressive instincts. We're asking you, I'm pleading with you to postpone stage three: the actual mass production of the hybrid. We need more time to perfect her."

"No Julie, my presentation last week was a smash hit. I have clients who've already invested largely on my guarantee that I can deliver herds in five years, and I always deliver. I can't break my word.

"We'll simply introduce tranquilizers into the livestock feed, simple solution for your concern. I'm tripling everyone's pay as a bonus for work well done."

Julie countered, "But doing that will pass the tranquilizers through for human consumption."

Maxwell retorted, "A tranquilized populace is a happy one in the eyes of the Elite. I already have the okay to continue, plus it was their recommendation.

"Now, proceed with stage three, and terminate stage one; the lab rats, because we have no further use for them. The speed at which they reproduce can't be allowed into the natural habitat, immediately destroy them. Ladies, and gentlemen, we've made it beyond the horizon, and it's going to be a beautiful day."

Julie lost the argument for the postponement of stage three, but she was elated on the decision to destroy the super rats. Julie hated these super aggressive laboratory specimens, especially King Rat.

Julie worked closely with rats during her career as a geneticist; it was a pre-functionary task of her profession to test all procedures first on lab rats before moving onto more complex specimens. These genetically tampered rats with hippo DNA were very mean, large, and strong. The super rats had managed to reproduce, and maintain the status without retrograding with smaller offspring; and that breakthrough was the key to proceeding with the domestics for stage three.

King Rat was the smartest, and most dangerous of the super rats, just putting him to death wouldn't be a deserved punishment. Julie wanted him to suffer with great anguish; it would suffice her hatred for the super rodent whom maimed her. Julie thumbed the stub of her pinky finger.

Julie darted the abnormally large rats with the air pistol, and death came instantly from the poison. She had them incinerated, a normal procedure when stretching the ethical envelope.

In the gloom of the mid-night she'd come back to carry out King Rat's death sentence, that's when all the techs would be gone, and only then she'd feel comfortable enough to finish the business between herself, and the great super rat.

Seldom Seen

A MOUSE DARTED THROUGH THE SLATS of the white picket fence in an attempt to save itself. It chanced a look back, and a black blur streaked overhead; just visible against a darkening sky.

In a single bound, the black tomcat vaulted the barrier. His hind legs projected him from the top of the fence to land ahead of the fleeing mouse. The cat landed with a muffled thud onto the turf, and spun to snare the rodent with a swipe of a clawed paw.

The mouse gambled, and lost, hoping the barrier would save its life from the black cat. Terror froze the mouse in the cat's grasp. The cat's head lunged forward, and the hunt was over. A bone-breaking crunch signaled the end of the mouse's life.

"OUTSTANDING!"

The black cat spun around with the mouse hanging from his jaws like a waterlogged cigar. Suddenly, Seldom Seen realized the chase took him into private property, a deadly mistake for a stray cat. Seldom Seen quickly glanced at the surroundings, and didn't detect any signs of a dog.

The black tomcat was in a huge yard. The grass, and shrubs were well manicured with bushes, flowerbeds dotting the landscape in planned patterns. The house was huge, a masterpiece of 30's architecture by a master, it stood solidly, and more than able to withstand a storm, or a cold winter's night. Farther ahead the black cat's senses zeroed in on the presence which applauded his hunting skills.

She spoke, "Come here."

Seldom Seen devoured the mouse with a few more bites. He sliced off the leathery tail with a clean bite as he got to the end of the quick meal.

Seldom Seen disliked swallowing rodent tails, because they tickled his throat.

Seldom Seen licked the inside edge of a paw, and caressed his head a few times. His tail in the air, Seldom Seen approached the other cat with feline curiosity. The black cat left paw prints on the concrete walkway as he exited the dewed turf. A screen door let in the summer breeze.

Starlight was a thoroughbred Persian. Seldom Seen looked at her, comparing himself with her exotic appearance. Seldom Seen was no teen, but she was quite more than a few years his senior, and only so because of her sheltered lifestyle. One of her eyes was lime green, and the other sky blue. Starlight's long coat fell perfectly into place from habitual brushing. A diamond-encrusted collar was her master's very expensive necklace now altered to fit loosely, but securely around her neck. When the Persian moved the collar shimmered like exploding fireworks. Starlight flexed, and her body responded in a way that makes the feline such a sensuous animal.

Mesmerized, Seldom Seen settled down in front of Starlight. He watched the humans beyond the doorway, and the activities there brought back fleeting memories of an earlier lifestyle. Seldom Seen felt a twinge of jealousy when he envisioned what Starlight's life must be like inside this abode.

Starlight leaned heavily against the screen that separated them. This was a rare opportunity for her to interact with a rogue.

Starlight licked her chops, "I hope that creature tasted better than it looked. Here in the house, I catch mice all the time, but I'd never eat one of the wretched things! I just play with them to pass the time, and then I release them. My name is Starlight. What's your name, do you have one?"

Starlight's tone was definitely upper crust, dripping with the trappings of high breeding.

"I have two names. In my previous lifestyle I was Cocoa. Now I go by the name Seldom Seen, and who are you, to let mice go free?"

Starlight purred softly, so delighted she could get a reaction. "I can do whatever I please! There's plenty of delicious chow, why would I ever want to ruin my appetite on hairy mice. They're so disgusting!"

No slang ever escaped her. Seldom Seen knew she never experienced street life.

Seldom Seen eyeballed Starlight with strong distaste. "You'd never survive out here where the going is very rough, and everything isn't handed to you in a bowl."

Seldom Seen flashed out a paw, and batted down a moth trying to break through the screen to the light inside the house. He pinned it to the concrete step.

She purred, "Are you challenging me?"

Starlight had been guaranteed her high standard of living for many years into the future. Starlight felt she'd certainly outlive this tomcat, even though she was much older; but her life would be a shallow one. Seldom Seen might die in a day, or a month from now, but his adventures on the streets made his life very rich.

Seldom Seen nodded, "Yes!"

Starlight made a soft purr, "I accept."

"Have you ever mothered kittens?" Seldom Seen was blunt, and to the point because it's the only way a stray survives on the streets. The black cat never looked directly into Starlight's big gorgeous eyes. Instead, he looked just beyond Starlight or, away from her; always on the alert for movement elsewhere. Death needed no calling card for the unwary.

The sheltered pedigree gazed upon the tomcat intensely without blinking, enthralled by him. "Yes, like me, they all are beautiful too."

Starlight licked her mouth. She wanted to devour Seldom Seen whole with the classy style of her pedigree.

The moth crunched as Seldom Seen ate it.

Starlight gazed, "It must be exciting to run free, to roam the streets, and go where you please. I envy you. Tell me what it's like to be on the other side, where there are no boundaries to block your path."

Seldom Seen flicked his tail a few times as he gathered his thoughts.

"First and foremost, it's a demanding lifestyle, and it's not for those like you." He waited for a negative reaction and found none.

As darkness crept over the early evening, Seldom Seen strung together many adventures about himself, and of others. Seldom Seen felt a strong energy between himself and Starlight, a tugging that registered on his heartstrings. Starlight was more than the ordinary felines who thrived on the streets. Her appearance alone dictated such thoughts, but Starlight's attitude was to the contrary, for an aristocrat she was very approachable.

Starlight listened with great fascination, purring softly when some of his predicaments amused her. She realized that a starving mental hunger was being filled in her mind. Starlight's idle thoughts vanished, and she was filled with warm memories from Seldom Seen's lives.

The black tomcat purred, "I must be on my way. I've got a lot more hunting to do if I'm not to go hungry tonight. I don't have your good fortune, goodbye!"

Starlight meowed, "WAIT!"

Seldom Seen slowed, and turned his right ear towards her.

"Why are you called Seldom Seen?"

He paused, "Because my coat's all black, and when I hunt at night; I'm seldom seen."

He darted into the darkness, and ended their conversation. Within a few meters of the door, he had vanished.

Starlight decided she liked the tomcat.

Starlight stood on her hindquarters and mewed, "PLEASE, come back!"

There was no answer.

"Will I ever see you again?" Starlight strained her keen vision against the shadows, finally glimpsing the gleam of his feline eyes reflecting the house lights back at her, and then his eyes disappeared, leaving her gloomier than the night that veiled him.

Starlight thought about the tomcat for a long time at the doorway. Seldom Seen's stories raced endlessly in her mind, and Starlight relived them as if they were her own adventures. Perhaps thoughts would bring him back, after all she'd been wishing for a visitor when he made the spectacular appearance.

Finally, she relinquished the possibility of his return when her master shut the door for the night. Starlight quickly traversed the well-traveled pathways of the house, which was her lifelong sanctuary.

Starlight jumped into her favorite place at the window. The curtains were drawn barring her eyes, so she crept around, and between the ferns that adorned the space.

Starlight peered into the darkness. No other cat had ever come to her house, only during her trips away; locked in a cage did she meet other felines at cat shows. She finally moved away. Expensive rugs cushioned her paw pads.

Starlight turned a corner, and was at her master's bedroom. Starlight paused at the entrance, and then gazed back the way she came. Warm thoughts of the tomcat dazzled her for a few moments, and then with some hesitation, jumped into Marlene's bed for the night. An arm drew her close. Starlight physically relaxed in the warm embrace of her protector, and provider, but mentally a black tomcat whizzed around in her mind at hurricane speed, shattering everything she'd come to know, and love.

Stars twinkled above. Seldom Seen continued his quest for a full stomach. The exchange with Starlight brought back some of his fondest adventures.

One very harsh winter, he stumbled across an abandoned warehouse after hunting a mouse that climbed through a broken window. He sat on the edge of the windowsill and peered beyond the slivers of shattered glass that were in the grooves. He saw a multitude of rodents going about their business of eating the moldy grain bursting through the burlap sacks.

Seldom Seen felt instantly rich. He carefully overcame the glass, and perched on the inside edge of the sill. The mice hadn't noticed him. It was dark, but for the eerie light of the full moon that cast his shadow onto the unsuspecting hordes below. He flexed one paw, unsheathing the claws repeatedly.

Thousands of mice scattered when he charged, but he netted one, and then another as he struck time after time. The feast continued for several minutes. Finally, he sat on the sill again, preparing to leave.

Seldom Seen's reign of terror ended when a big silver gray tomcat encroached on his territory, and chased him away. Other stray cats had disappeared during that harsh winter when food was scarce. Seldom Seen was lucky enough to stumble onto such a fortune, and survive. Something beckoned him to follow that mouse instead of slaying it immediately.

Barring mishap; Seldom Seen should live a few more years, but eventually time and circumstances would beat him into the ground forever. During next spring, and summer, new kittens would emerge to replace the dead, and dying cats, some of them would be his offspring. Seldom Seen was a player in that never-ending replenishment of life on the streets. One day, some of his offspring when mature would challenge and defeat him, and they would reign over what he now mastered.

Seldom Seen paused at one of his marked trails that led away from the suburbs. He ventured into a field of tall grass. His pupils were fully dilated. The encounter with Starlight a few hours earlier left him filled with restless energy. Seldom Seen paused for a moment to clean his satiny black coat. Nature provided all he needed for survival whether man-made, or in the wilderness.

With a change of attitude, he began stalking in the lush grass looking for any movement, or sound that might betray a mouse. A rustle just ahead brought him into a crouch; an unwary field mouse was foraging for seeds. The mouse unknowingly came to Seldom Seen.

Seldom Seen slew it with one swipe, and a bite. As he snipped the mouse's tail off the hunger in his stomach was silenced, but the incident brought another vision of Starlight to his mind. The new hunger he couldn't satisfy.

After a profitable evening of hunting, Seldom Seen began his trek back to his lair. During the journey through the city dump, he saw a crowd of rodents gathered around one monstrously large white rat. The rat was elevated higher than the rest on the top of a vintage sedan. King Rat had their attention. Seldom Seen crept closer, climbing to the top of a bulldozed mountain of trash to get a high angle of this great event.

The super rat spat trash from his full cheeks. "I was very fortunate tonight, for I have defeated two of our great adversaries, and only minutes apart. I foiled the plans of my creator, who sought to kill me, and then I destroyed the newborns of a stray cat that left her unattended brood. This is how I arrive to you, on the wings of glorious victories!"

King Rat peered at his new followers. His squeaky voice boomed with confidence. He was huge, more than a match for any domestic cat. King Rat had delivered himself from destruction. King Rat was the result of generations of gene tampering; the experiment had been so successful he was able to overpower a human with wit, and strength.

Throughout the dump for as long as any of its denizens could remember, was a legend of a savior who would redeem the lost, and mend the broken. One who'd gather them up, and move them far beyond their natural standards. King Rat was that prophecy coming true. His plan was to lead all rodents into a final battle for supremacy for the earth. Tonight, those who were banished to the city dump saw King Rat as the one to fulfill that goal.

The night was crystal clear, and bats fluttered across the full moon on leathery wings echoing their high-pitched screeches. Seldom Seen listened as King Rat whipped the mob with hatred, "Seven tiny kittens, they were newborn, no more than a few days old. I butchered all of them!"

King Rat's snout was red with blood, and shredded flesh ejected from his stuffed cheeks as he continued, "We've lived the dark life for too long, shunned by Man. We are the outcasts, but no more! Why hide from the daylight, it belongs to us too! Journey with me, for I will lift us from every hellhole!"

King Rat saw it, a black shadow launching itself towards him. Before his followers could react, Seldom Seen struck the super rat, lashing out a paw stroke. King Rat rolled off the roof of the car, an eyeball ripped from his head from the cat's stiletto claws.

Seldom Seen's actions were automatic, because cat, and rat had been mortal enemies for a hundred thousand centuries. Most stray cats avoided the dump at night for fear of being bitten by a rabid varmint, but the dump had always been good hunting for Seldom Seen. He was angry because of the senseless slaughter of innocent newborns by this fiend.

A horde of rats formed an arena of doom around him. Hurt and dazed, King rat squared off against this assassin. Seldom Seen realized what his hasty actions had done. Seldom Seen's hiss boomed like thunder, and then he attacked any rats that dare move within range of his sharp paw strikes.

With his good eye, King Rat saw Seldom Seen charge after puffing up. Seldom Seen hooked his claws into King Rat, and they disappeared beneath the trash locked in combat. He felt the super strength of King Rat as they grappled unseen under the trash. The ring of rodents went into the trash, not waiting for them to resurface.

Seldom Seen's fangs sank into King Rat's neck trying to sever the spinal cord, but the rat was too muscular for his fangs to reach the vital nerve column. They emerged on top again, and broke apart. Many rats rushed to them, surrounding the two with the ebb, and flow of battle. They gave room as needed for King Rat to fight unimpeded.

Seldom Seen re-evaluated his tactics, and determined his advantage was his reach. With a flurry of paw strikes, he ripped King Rat's coat into streaks of crimson. Ears laid back, and lips snarling to reveal reddened fangs. Seldom Seen paused wide-eyed, and crazed from the fight.

King Rat felt the torture of the cat's claws, and again he went down under a barrage of cutting paw strikes. King Rat fought the cat, but he was no match for Seldom Seen's mid-range weaponry. Sensing trouble, the ring of rats closed in on the duelist. Seldom Seen was now over-whelmed and in trouble. He received several bites in his sides and legs, and he was overthrown by the sheer numbers that swarmed him, and still more rats came running from every crevice of the dump to force their way into the fight. With faltering strength the tomcat battled his way out of the throng with a terrific flurry of paw strikes, and then vanished into the night. Only a distant meow gave token of his presence.

Seldom Seen yowled, "I punished you tonight, if only I could've killed you!

"Let it be known to all, that Seldom Seen spilled your blood tonight, but next time I will kill you because of your horrible crime." After the echoes faded, there was silence.

King Rat slowly righted himself, making a puddle of blood where he rested. King Rat vowed to find this tomcat, and get revenge. Blood soiled his white coat, and his destroyed eye made him dizzy, it lay crushed in the trash. Seldom Seen's name was stamped into King Rat's brain; this cat was very brave, but King Rat realized he'd never kill the cat in wide-open spaces like the dump. He'd have to corner the fast cat in a tight spot where his bulk and strength would make the advantage in his favor.

With death a real possibility, he immediately began the actions that would set his grand design into motion. King Rat's concubines addressed him all night, and in turn they would birth litters, and they in turn would unleash an unchecked horde of super rodents.

Seldom Seen was at the entrance of his secondary lair, and there was no sign of Tink. He moved inside, and saw the destroyed bodies of their newborn litter. King Rat had destroyed his offspring!

They were tore into pieces of shredded flesh, and fur, each one was a mass of mush; it took time to kill so thoroughly. Tink had abandoned the litter, and when Seldom Seen came out of the liar; he was a broken cat.

He ran away, wanting to forget this tragedy. Tink had left their offspring unprotected during his hunting spree, and that was unforgivable; it was on her watch the kittens were killed. Seldom Seen quit her, and the selfish ways of the greedy feline, for it had cost him dearly. Starlight was the answer to soothe this tragedy.

Seldom Seen nestled in the forked branches of an oak tree to sleep away the rest of the night. He was safe, hidden by thousands of leaves blocking the sky, the ground, and everything else from view.

He'd definitely get revenge on King Rat; a fight to the death.

Now, other thoughts pressed Seldom Seen; with ears laid back he purred to the Moon, and put himself into a hypnotic trance.

Perhaps he'd die as an old alley cat, looking for scraps among the dreaded rats. No alley cat lived long in the city dump. Maybe he'd succumb to a crushing death beneath the tires of a fast auto while still strong, and virile. Neither prospect was ideal.

Every day he feared such thoughts and they'd always return to deeply haunt him. He was born into a household. It was his birthright, but now he was on the streets with no safety in his future. Seldom Seen's head bobbed as he groomed himself, licking his chest, and forelegs. An owl hooted in the distance but he ignored it like all the natural night sounds. He nodded into a light sleep with thoughts of Starlight giving his existence hope.

Starlight was up the next morning, and relaxing on the soft black leather sofa in a darkened corner of the expansive house; it seemed that even the sofa could conjure memories of the black cat. Beside her was Marlene, and a brass floor lamp was lit for cozy reading. Starlight often used this spot to catnap, and daydream her life away in Marlene's soft embrace.

Finally, Starlight took her daily post among the ferns, and other plants at the large bay window. There, she could view the outside world with endless fascination.

Starlight gazed across the green expanse of grass seeking movement, searching for a glimpse of Seldom Seen. Rays of the morning sunlight struck back at her through the window, giving the disarray of her coat an aura like radiance.

She remembered every detail of the encounter with Seldom Seen last night. He was the most adventurous feline she'd ever met. Seldom Seen certainly was a different kind of cat then she'd been accustomed to. Starlight confessed that he had a different quality then the other males she'd competed against and defeated, definitely a rogue!

While thinking about how interesting his life must be, Starlight realized how dull her own lifestyle was, and those facts deeply saddened her. Ever since Starlight's birth, her days were long, and uneventful. Starlight experienced nothing new, or in the least bit interesting, and if something different did occur, it was cheapened, because it wasn't through her own deliberate action, but because of Marlene's actions.

After waiting for a long time for Seldom Seen, she crept away for some nourishment. Starlight turned the corner into the kitchen, and she saw a mouse casually inching its way along the linoleum without fear. Starlight sat, and watched the gray rodent in a new way.

Toadflax saw Starlight, but wasn't alarmed. He frolicked often in Starlight's paws without being in danger. Starlight was weak, un-attuned to the ways of the stray cat's philosophy. The mouse often bragged to his fellows about her, but none were bold enough to play with their natural enemy as he did. Toadflax had no time for play because he was hungry. The mouse squeaked to reassure Starlight of his intentions. Starlight watched as he inched to the chow bowl to eat.

Starlight thought of Seldom Seen, and the tip of her tail flicked. How swift and agile he'd been for the kill. He'd never let such an easy catch escape. Something was happening to Starlight; it was a new feeling that welled up from deep within.

Finished eating Toadflax began to scurry back the way he'd came, oblivious to Starlight's changing awareness. Toadflax paused to clean his whiskers.

Flashbacks came vividly to Starlight of the moment when Seldom Seen caught the field mouse, and killed it. She remembered the terror in its black eyes just before it died. Starlight crouched, and prepared to attack. The ancient fires were reignited. She wanted to taste what Seldom Seen ate.

Outside, the summer Sun weakened behind a bank of clouds. The bright morning sky of a few minutes ago was becoming cloudy for a mid-afternoon shower.

Toadflax looked at Starlight, and froze. The sparkle in Starlight's eyes told him that she was re-made, because an event had changed her; a flash second later the mouse was dying in her jaws. Starlight sank her fangs into the mouse, until she tasted its sweet warm blood. He wiggled fiercely to get out. Several bones cracked, and then a squirt of crimson soiled Starlight's coat as her jaws popped his guts open. Toadflax died.

Unknowingly, Toadflax forfeited his life to start Starlight's new adventure. Starlight devoured the mouse, and that moment forward she accepted Seldom Seen's challenge in earnest; and vowed to escape the cozy sanctuary, and venture into Seldom Seen's world.

INSIDE A GARBAGE CAN FAR from her home, Starlight heard the pleasant sound of tinkling bells. Starlight stopped to listen, wondering what could possibly make such a pleasant sound from such a putrid place. Starlight hadn't eaten in days, and wondered if she made a mistake in escaping from Marlene. It was a lot harder to snare wild mice than tame ones.

Tink leaped from the weathered garbage can with a half-devoured turkey drumstick in her jaws. Tink landed on the pavement accompanied by a melody from the tin bells attached to her collar. Bells once meant to shine were now tarnished with ancient stains. These bells insured sorrow for Tink's life on the streets, betraying her most adept approaches while hunting mice, warning them to flee before she could reach a killing zone. This young and agile feline was doomed to the lifestyle of an old alley cat while still in her prime. Tink's gluttony for dining exclusively on human leftovers added many ounces to her frame too, but she was not unattractive.

Tink looked at the newcomer, "There's plenty more. Help yourself, are you hungry?"

Tink tore a dried scrap of the turkey from the bone, and devoured it with relentless bites. Flies were everywhere, attracted by the odor of rotting food.

Starlight wondered if she saw a vision of herself, it wasn't the lifestyle she'd envisioned. Ever since the escape she hadn't any excitement, or adventure. Everything she visualized about street life had yet to materialize. Starlight wondered if it existed at all. Perhaps Seldom Seen had teased her, and she wholeheartedly believed him. Starlight felt very disappointed in her efforts to find the thrilling lifestyle the black cat described.

Hunger pangs brought her back to reality. Starlight jumped into the muck with a lithe leap, making a swarm of flies rise before settling down again. Starlight hadn't been able to find Seldom Seen since her escape. She didn't know where to begin looking for him. This new culture was very alien to her. She also didn't know how to find her way home. The decision to run away had unerringly become final.

Starlight snatched up a piece of bone, and bounded out of the can; damning herself for being tricked so easily by Seldom Seen. Starlight landed beside the tabby, dropped her morsel, and picked at it. She wasn't accustomed to seeing crawling creatures on her food.

Tink pawed at the sparkling diamond collar around Starlight's neck. It sparkled constantly as Starlight went about the tedious procedure of avoiding the maggots on her infested morsel.

"You're new around here aren't you? I know all the cats that roam these streets."

Starlight perked up.

"I see you're not as majestic as you appear, Long Hair." Tink pawed the collar again. Tink realized the newcomer was trapped in the same predicament as herself. A mouse could just as easily see the sparkle of a streetlight, or a full moon off the diamond facets, and that was the dominator between herself and this thoroughbred, and that fact gave them a common problem.

Starlight bit off a sliver of gristle, and swallowed it. "Perhaps you know a particular tomcat I'm looking for."

Tink smiled, "Who?"

"Cocoa, do you know him?"

Tink was puzzled. "That's strange because it means nothing. I don't know any tomcat that goes by that name."

Tink turned away to leap into the garbage can again.

"WAIT! You probably know him as Seldom Seen!"

Tink immediately flexed her whiskers, "Oh, that scoundrel! Why waste your time seeking him out when there's so much else to do."

"He owes me."

Tink was surprised, "The Dukes owe no one anything around here. They take what fancies them, and that's all to it. You're deeply mistaken if you think you can get anything from him, in fact from any tomcat."

"Don't judge me by your own ineptness, can you find him?"

Tink smiled, "You're all that, huh?"

"Yes, I'm that, and more!"

Tink smiled, what a fool she thought about this newcomer, "Ah yes! The Black Duke of Tewksbury, quadrant two in this neighborhood, in order to find him you must seek the wisdom of Wisecat. He, and Wisecat are strong allies. I can easily find Wisecat. She never goes anywhere. Come with me."

The last few days of Starlight's anguished life fell away and her hopes brightened, and she forgot the hunger in her stomach.

She meowed, "Let's go!"

They raced off accompanied by Tink's tingling bells. Starlight's heart almost burst in her chest as they dashed towards a new destination. They eventually arrived at a large oak tree; the abandoned house beside was the home of Wisecat. The house stood solid though in lonely ruin with its roof partially caved in, and its windows boarded up. Above, at the front of the house was an attic window which let in a little of the outside world.

They climbed the mighty oak with Tink leading the way. They leaped onto the pitched roof, and moved toward the entrance through the timbers. Tink led the beautiful newcomer into the burned structure with cautious steps.

Inside was lofty, and cool, just the right abode for someone named Wisecat. Their eyes quickly grew accustomed to the mildewed darkness. There, sitting in the attic window was Wisecat, a purebred Siamese, and as old as any cat could hope to be.

WISECAT TURNED TOWARDS THE VISITORS, and gave them a blank stare. She was nearly blinded by cataracts, and couldn't make out their forms in the shadows. Wisecat was a frail cat, but wisdom made her one of the strongest cats to breathe mother earth's air.

Starlight saw the aged feline's only weakness, and turned to Tink, "How can a blind cat help me find Cocoa?"

"Cocoa?" Wisecat asked.

"I was the only one who knew him by that name."

"O great one, I bring a newcomer. Starlight is of the long hair, and I've never seen her kind before, but she asks questions I can't answer, so I brought her to you."

Wisecat paused, and then yawned. Starlight and Tink sat quietly waiting for a response. The Persian eyed the surroundings; it was odorless, and tasteless, barren of everyday life. Ghostly cobwebs hung through the vast space. Near the front, all light came from the attic window as they sat near it. In some respects, it reminded Starlight of her home in Tavenry.

Tink had been here many times. Any cat that thrived on the streets eventually met Wisecat. Some came more often than others, depending on the primary goal of their lifestyle. Wisecat was one of the many doorways to the source of life on the streets.

"Tink, it's been too long since your last visit. Is everything fine with you?"

The tabby vigorously shook her head. "Have you figured out a way to free me from this noise maker? I hate it!"

"Ah yes, the bells around your neck, if not for them, then how would I recognize you?" Wisecat had contemplated long over Tink's dilemma.

"A human has imprisoned you with sound, and only a human can release you from it."

Tink was saddened. Tink's last hope was gone. Her fate was sealed. Starlight's emotions were jolted by Tink's reaction, plus it wasn't fair that her new acquaintance should suffer so.

"Why must she live like this, and who are you?"

Wisecat blindly looked upon Starlight, "And you, why do you seek another when so much must be learned about yourself first?"

"What do you mean?" Starlight replied.

Wisecat flexed her ancient muscles. Tink relaxed, and listened, prepared to hear wisdom. Wisecat cleaned her long, elegant whiskers, always her opening gesture before a long speech.

"Listen Starlight, and know what all cats must know before they pass into the beyond. Long ago, not even I can fathom the date; our species appeared on the earth. We were ordinary creatures, not to be loved, or hated. We hunted for food, and grew accustomed to our rough lifestyle. We carved out a niche in nature, and asked for nothing we didn't earn."

Wisecat paused a long time to gather more thoughts, and neither Tink, nor Starlight dare interrupt her deep meditation.

"Back then, there were others who were different, the rats. We chose the wise and correct pathway, while the rats sought devious routes. Their evil thoughts transformed them into their current form. They flourish where others refuse. Their lives are cursed by darkness, and they rarely see a bright summer day.

"They are poisoned by the humans to this day, and yet humans love, and embrace us into their homes. The rodent's only defense against extinction is its ability to multiply more rapidly than they are destroyed. They have a resourcefulness to multiply that can't be defeated.

"Because we toiled hard and long, the ancient goddess Bastet granted two favors to all cats. First, a life of leisure among the humans, and the most precious of all, nine lives to do with as we please.

"Each of us starts a new life upon a change in lifestyle. Never make a foolish change, because once taken it is forever lost, but you do start with nine. Remember that number, nine.

"Be sure to profit from each life you set aside." Wisecat stared with nearly blind eyes at Starlight for a long while to emphasize that point.

It dawned on Starlight. She'd just started a new lifestyle.

"A lifestyle can last any length of time, from short minutes to long years, but as long as you have a remaining life, then you will not physically die. Once you enter into your ninth life, only then can physical death embrace you, and take you. The key is to learn wisdom from every lifestyle you set aside, so that you may have a higher form of life when your life-force reincarnates, understand?"

Starlight was swimming in a dense fog of information. Tink nodded in and out of slumber.

Wisecat closed, "It's a cherished custom among the strays to shed our old names and take on a new one as a gesture upon entering a new lifestyle."

Tink broke in, "I beg your pardon for interrupting, but she is as fluffy, and distant as the clouds that float beyond our reach. Let her be known as Cloudy, because with time she'll vanish, just like the clouds overhead."

"Then Cloudy it shall be."

Before Starlight could protest, Wisecat christened her new lifestyle with a lick between her gorgeous eyes.

"What about Seldom Seen? In an indirect way he's the cause of my new beginning. Please tell me how to find him."

Wisecat stretched out her body, and moved to the warmth of the attic window. "To find him, you must hunger the night, because that's where he thrives."

I<small>T WAS A BEAUTIFUL MORNING.</small> The sky took on a surrealistic dawn with feathering clouds reflecting the orange and blue sunrise. Rays of sunlight broke out from behind a group of clouds that drifted low on the horizon streaking the sky with laser-like beams. Songbirds warmed the air with a multiplicity of melodies.

Seldom Seen paused at the picket fence, and peered between the slats. At eye level, the three-story house seemed like a gigantic fortress in a savanna of neatly trimmed grass. Convinced there was no danger, he leaped onto the narrow fence and sat. From this elevated angle he sought a way to penetrate the big house, and get her.

Seldom Seen groomed himself waiting a long time. The Sun raised higher, its rays evaporating the morning dew. Directly ahead was a monumental task. Starlight had become a shadow of a memory, a remembrance of a delightful experience. Seldom Seen was rash to leave her. He was willing to do anything to be with Starlight now. During the past few days, it seemed his life was out of control. A happenstance meeting had altered his life forever, and that realization shocked him. Hunger pangs reminded Seldom Seen of what he should be doing, but he sat like a sentinel, and watched the house.

A door opened, it was the same door in which he met Starlight. Seldom Seen eased from his perch like a diving falcon, and hit the ground running. Throwing all caution away he approached the doorway with a loud meow.

Marlene set the steaming tea kettle onto the stove. She heard the meow, and thought her beloved Persian had finally come home. Marlene wondered what possessed Starlight to run off into the unknown. Two days without her feline was enough torture. Starlight had dashed past Marlene, and out the opened doorway when she retrieved the morning newspaper, and that act left the elderly woman very shaken.

Marlene loved cats since childhood. Starlight was now queen, and a champion Persian bred from a line that went hand-in-hand with her own family's lineage. Marlene planned to defend her ribbon with Starlight in two months at the national cat show.

Marlene wasn't concerned about the necklace, because it was insured. Once the papers were sent off she'd be reimbursed. Now, suddenly Marlene's trepidation disappeared as she heard the meowing at the back door. That was one of Starlight's favorite spots.

Seldom Seen kept meowing, and calling out for Starlight. As Marlene approached to open the door, he fled, and then stopped as Marlene's soothing voice connected with his instinctive nature to be loved by a human.

Marlene knelt to the black tomcat, and lifted him to her bosom. Seldom Seen relaxed in her warm, soft embrace. The tender tones of her voice made him purr. She rubbed his head, and stepped into the kitchen.

"Are you hungry my friend?" Marlene set him down before Starlight's empty chow bowl. "Let's see what I can muster up."

Seldom Seen stretched a few times, bits of his previous lifestyle rushed on him with vivid memory. The aroma of a freshly opened can of tuna sent waves of excitement through him. He went to Marlene, caressing her ankles with his flanks, and uttering meek meows.

Marlene forked chunks of the tuna into Starlight's bowl, and Seldom Seen savored every bite. Marlene watched him consume the meal. Seldom Seen couldn't match Starlight in beauty, but he could temporarily satisfy her need for a cat. Marlene sat at the table, and sipped her tea. "Well, my curious friend, what brings you to my doorstep this morning?"

Seldom Seen twitched an ear to her voice, wondering what she was saying.

Marlene spoke, "Perhaps you've seen my precious feline during your travels. If you do, would you please bring her home to me?"

The plain knowledge that Starlight ate from this spot was a hollow victory. Seldom Seen's cat sense told him Starlight was long gone. Her fresh scent had vanished.

Sᴇʟᴅᴏᴍ Sᴇᴇɴ ɢᴀᴢᴇᴅ ᴜᴘᴏɴ ᴍᴀɴʏ rooftops. The shimmering heat waves gave the roof an aquatic appearance. He'd been to the roof many times via the oak. He once lived inside the shell of the old house when it thrived with life. That memory was still alive in him from a previous lifestyle. The boarded-up house made a perfect home for old Wisecat. With Seldom Seen's help, the Siamese never had to venture forth onto the hostile streets. Both strays were bonded to the house, the younger one by an earlier lifestyle, and the older one by being shielded from harsh weather, and dangers of the streets.

Seldom Seen liked to roam the night, looking for action, and adventure on the tar and grass. Being locked up in solitude was no longer his lifestyle. He peered into the hole of the burned-out roof, and then looked across his territory.

Starlight was out there somewhere. He'd never thought such a pristine cat would be adventurous enough to runoff into the unknown. Seldom Seen had misjudged her, and now it cost him dearly with his budding emotions. The stories about him were enough to ignite the fire behind those big soft Persian eyes. He vowed to never misjudge Starlight again.

Seldom Seen pondered his life, and as usual; it took a whimsical turn. Outwardly, he'd done all he could to track Starlight, but fate placed an unmanageable curve in his path. Starlight had crossed into his world, and she had vanished.

Seldom Seen was bone tired, and most of all, very restless. After leaving Marlene, he continued the search for Starlight. Seldom Seen usually would've been content knowing he'd done all that was possible,

21

but his uneasiness grew stronger, making him feel weaker. In such times he turned to Wisecat. Seldom Seen moved from the bright sunlight, and into the dank environment inside the attic.

Cloudy's curiosity about life expanded as she rethought what Wisecat said to her. From ancient times, a civilization on the Nile River placed felines on pedestals, and brought them permanently into the hearts of humans by domesticating them.

Cloudy would've never known her species history if not for the drastic action of escaping from Marlene. Cloudy had regained the history kept from her because of imprisonment, and felt content knowing she acted properly to run away. Her stomach growled from hunger though, and she hadn't purred in days. Cloudy lost weight which wasn't ideal, because she'd never been an over-weight feline. Marlene paid strict attention to her diet. She'd been as healthy as any champion could attain.

Cloudy was still a novice at catching mice, and she depended on the garbage cans of the humans for her nourishment. Much to Cloudy's dismay, she grew accustomed to foraging in the trash more, and hunting less. Before moving on, Tink taught Cloudy a few tricks about foraging through trash. The best bites were usually the hardest to attain, early in the morning before dawn, and sometimes after dusk when humans put the garbage on the curb for removal. Tink taught Cloudy to look for sealed items. Although hard to get at, such food wasn't tainted with sickening bacteria. Tink told Cloudy of times when she was ill with diarrhea from eating bites that were filled with germs. Tink also added that maggots didn't taste all that bad. The healthiest bites of food were of course, alive, it was the only way to measure freshness and never, ever eat a dead animal unless killed through your own actions. All these rules were the philosophy of the alley cat.

Tink added a special warning not to forage in the large *Dumpsters* usually found behind restaurants, and apartment complexes. Those were definitely owned by a tomcat, more specifically a Duke. Only in extreme hunger would another cat, other than the Duke of the turf go there to feed. It was better to starve through the bad times until one's luck changed than receive a royal beating.

Cloudy approached a *Dumpster* located behind Manny's restaurant. Cloudy paused; she never experienced such a deep hunger. The restaurant had a good turnover last night, and strong aromas from the put out garbage traveled the warm breeze. Cloudy looked up to the top edge of the steel monstrosity, remembering Tink's warning about the *Dumpsters,* and the tomcats. Perhaps she was on Seldom Seen's turf. With that premonition, she coiled, and then leaped onto the edge of the bin. Cloudy looked at the trash piled halfway to the top. Scraps of cooked steak, potatoes, and other vegetables were tossed in, along with paper from the previous night's tabletops. All she cared about was meat. There were only a few maggots, and flies, but not like she'd grown accustomed; it was surely a Duke's treasure chest.

In she went, grabbing a large piece of rare sirloin. It was still tender with blood. As Cloudy ate it, thoughts of Marlene, and how she'd depended on her for food began to vanish. Cloudy was proud to be able to feed herself now. She just wished it were more consistent. With every passing hour Marlene faded further into the past, a lifestyle to be forgotten. After only a few days Cloudy got used to the absence of a warm bed, and being brushed by a loving hand. Cloudy looked up, and saw a Duke spying on her.

Never had he seen such beauty. The calico tabby jumped down into the trash beside her, making Cloudy rear back. He circled Cloudy checking her from every angle. The tri-colored tomcat had a sadistic approach to life. His coat displayed his hard-style philosophy with many scars of missing fur. A broken tail bent at an angle exemplified his determination to endure any pain to get what he wanted. Raw courage, and perseverance earned him the appropriate name, Moxie.

Cloudy moved back, finally retreating to the top edge of the *Dumpster* seeking escape. She was ready to flee, but couldn't when Moxie followed her to the edge in hot pursuit. Cloudy stopped, feeling the pressure of his eyes. Each time their eyes locked, it confirmed his inner strength, and cat sense. Moxie was a cat's cat.

To Cloudy, he was very young, and tough. Cloudy was accustomed to an elegant cat's courting style. Cloudy saw in Moxie the brutality, and destructiveness of an earthquake. She felt terror by being so close to him, but that stimulated Cloudy with excitement, and that was what she truly desired by coming out here. Without realizing, she surrendered without protest. Moxie's orange eyes bored into her blue and green eyes with strong passion. He bit into the back of her neck, and without preliminaries, fucked her. Moxie was definitely a rogue.

Tutulem reached the attic, and saw two cats conversing at the window. The mouse scurried into a small crevice, his heart racing from fear, and also success. He found the black cat! His head popped up again. The black cat hadn't seen him. King Rat would be pleased with the news.

King Rat sent legions of mice out to locate Seldom Seen. His fever for revenge was still hot, and mice were his main tools for information gathering. Tutulem was his best spy, at times risking his life just like now. Something special was going on. Tutulem suppressed his fear, and moved closer. The words he heard almost made his heart stop.

Wisecat spoke, "King Rat must be executed, and every second he lives threatens us."

Seldom Seen groomed himself as Wisecat continued. "I've had several visions from the source. If the super rat is successful with his master plan, then the world will be changed for the worst. I hope it's not already too late. The humans have created a freak, and his kind must never be allowed to multiply."

Seldom Seen looked out the dirty window at the noon Sun. His body was set like an anchor, but his mind drifted in, and out of Wisecat's wisdom like a piece of driftwood wrestling with the waves on the shore for purchase.

"King Rat seeks your hide, and when he finds you, he must embrace his own end, not yours. You are the chosen one." Wisecat was finished.

Seldom Seen thought about that. He was being forced into a titanic struggle of good against evil. He would be the hammer that could mold their victory. Seldom Seen gazed out the portal. Wisecat was more than a friend. Over the years she had been a teacher, and a pillar of strength for him. Seldom Seen admitted that he owed all his cunning cat sense to this very cat. He had been forced into the streets at a young age, and it was Wisecat who taught the starving kitten how to survive. Her wisdom had always been sound but today, her hallowed words rang hollow. Seldom Seen had another problem to work out, and it seemed much more important than King Rat.

Moxie groomed a paw, and gazed upon the beauty he had ravished. Cloudy gathered her courage. She eyed the Duke cautiously, wary for more aggressive actions. Moxie was good-looking, but only in a rough way. By far his strongest assets didn't lie there. Cloudy felt the reckless and dangerous attitude he possessed, which is what made her interested in him. Cloudy did a body lengthening stretch. Cloudy now strengthened, a moment earlier she'd been conquered.

Cloudy hopped down into the *Dumpster* again, and searched in the trash. "There are plenty of good bites here. Surely you don't mind sharing."

Moxie eyed her with contempt, whiskers flaring. First she stole from him, and then told him how to run his turf. Cloudy was within range to receive his wrath, but Moxie didn't attack her. He realized she was something very special.

Cloudy spotted another juicy hunk of steak, and leaped after it. With her tiny paw placed on top of it Cloudy made an offering to Moxie. Moxie smiled his famous confident smile, the one he wore with victory assured.

Moxie landed beside her, and took the bite into his mouth, eating it quickly. Moxie wondered where she came from; this exotic feline who was at home in a bin of garbage. During the few minutes of interaction Moxie had forced his will on Cloudy. She was Moxie's possession.

Moxie pawed the necklace. "These bites are nothing. I'll treat you to some real fresh stuff. Follow me."

Moxie hopped to the edge of the bin, and down to the ground, and then looked up. Cloudy responded, and repeated his maneuver to the ground.

It was noon, inside Manny's kitchen; the chef and owner of this bodega and restaurant would be cooking up a storm of orders for the lunchtime crowd. Every day, Moxie made it a point to appear at the back door. Today he was rewarded with a delicacy that Manny couldn't provide. Any ordinary stray would've received his immediate brutality for trespassing into quadrant one; his turf, and then stealing from him; but Cloudy was beautiful. She was extraordinary. Cloudy was a prize any tomcat would want offspring from, and Moxie had just made a deposit in her.

Moxie went through the split screen of the door. Inside the kitchen, the rattle of pots and pans clanged with controlled violence. Manny sweated over the stoves, adding flavorings to his recipes with a few ripe curses. He looked up as Moxie came in through the ripped screen door.

"What you want Romeo? Can't you see I'm busy? You're coming too early again." The meat cleaver came down with a precise chop, and he tossed a sliver of raw beef to the tomcat.

Moxie caught the morsel and ate it, and then meowed for more. Manny grunted, "Romeo, you should've been a dog! Maybe then you'd earn your keep around here. What the hell good are you for? Every day you come in here and eat the best I have to offer. I should have it so good!"

Manny gave a gutsy laugh and tossed Moxie another sliver of beef.

Manny was the closest thing Moxie had as a master. The lonely cook told the cat his problems, and then posed his own workable solutions as he cleaned up after serving the late dinners. The self-induced therapy had built up his restaurant business. As long as Moxie showed up, the tomcat would never go hungry. Moxie had the pleasure of a double lifestyle. Their relationship worked well because he ate regularly, and without the penalty of being locked indoors like most house cats.

"I remember the first time you poked your head in here. My cooking smells that good, huh, well thank you!" Manny had deep admiration for the nicked-up tomcat. In the beginning, when he first opened for business many tomcats fought vicious battles to win possession of the newly placed *Dumpster*. When a tomcat won, there'd be another ready to challenge the winner, and then Moxie arrived.

Manny remembered the first time the barbaric tomcat fought for possession of the *Dumpster*. He'd been a scrawny thing then, but his determination to win at all costs was very strong. Moxie traded fierce paw strokes with an angry silver-gray tomcat named Bossy who had flashing yellow eyes. Manny watched; an iron frying pan held firm in his hand. Manny was drunk from drinking with the waiters over the celebration of opening week, and had come out to silence the racket outside his kitchen door. He stopped to watch the cats duke it out over the *Dumpster.*

It reminded Manny of his own youth when he'd been a tough, knife-wielding teen in the gangs fighting to protect their territory. That was a long time ago, but it all came rushing back as he watched the two tomcats fight for mastership of the *Dumpster;* and Duke Status. Neither cat rushed into harm's way, but challenged one another with cautious respect. For Manny the weapons were razors, now he witnessed the respect of two tomcats in a darkened alleyway go tooth and claw.

Bossy was the present master of this new place, and was sure to win because of his wisdom and strength. Bossy had maintained the rights for three nights running. Moxie showed up as the teen that would tumble the seasoned master; for Bossy had many offspring claiming his silver-grey coat.

Manny heaved the frying pan at the two tomcats, and it separated them with a hard thump. Bossy fled into the darkness of the alleyway. Manny leaned over the calico cat. Moxie lay still with his tiny tongue hanging from the side of his mouth, and eyes glazed over. Manny grabbed the tomcat by the scruff of the neck, and tossed him into the *Dumpster.* Thinking he killed the rouge cat.

Moxie woke a few minutes later, and shook his head to clear it. A sharp pain registered from his broken tail, it bent sharply at one point halfway down its length. A broken leg would've been fatal; at least he could endure this pain without missing a meal. He ate heartily, and then went off to recuperate for tomorrow night's fights. Whosoever won the most battles gradually beat it into the heads of the other tomcats; the right to claim the *Dumpster* as new turf. Moxie, the young upstart was determined it would be him.

As Manny dumped the last garbage of dinner trash into the bin, he was surprised to see the calico cat move just beyond the streetlamp's light. There was no fear in Moxie's glowing eyes, only caution, and respect from the earlier event.

Manny had to laugh, "One tough bandito!"

Manny had been serving up dinners inside, while Moxie opened up a can of whip-ass outside. He had won the treasures Manny brought out to him; perhaps Bossy had been more injured than Moxie for he never reappeared at this site. Every night thereafter, Moxie reigned supreme until no other's dared to trespass on his new turf. A young cat turned Duke with this newly won turf, and before his time.

In came Cloudy through the broken screen. Manny scratched his balding scalp. "What the hell you got there, Romeo? You got a steady girlfriend now?"

Manny pulled the skillet away from the roaring flame, and moved out from behind the cook station. "You're so sly, and she's high class too!"

Manny looked at Cloudy. "You hungry honey?"

He saw the diamond necklace around Cloudy's neck. "Wait a second! That cat's got diamond jewelry!"

Manny hurried to get at the filet on the cutting board, and then shook it to get her attention.

Manny drew Cloudy in with the bait, and patted her large head; easing his greasy fingers onto the necklace. He tossed the filet to Moxie, "You earned it Romeo!

"These diamonds are real! You got a real rich girlfriend!" Manny yanked Cloudy over his head like a hooked fish by the necklace, and shook her as if in a noose.

"I got you!"

Cloudy puffed up, and hissed to free herself. Moxie lunged at Manny's face, making him drop Cloudy. She landed on all fours and ran towards the split screen door. Manny fell backwards as he tried to avoid the swiping claws of Moxie, but he had the diamond necklace firmly in his hand as he tried to fend off the tomcat. Moxie swelled with anger.

Manny held onto the diamonds as he frantically pulled the enraged tomcat off his face with a scream. Manny threw the cat through the hanging pans and utensils, but Moxie merely landed upright, and charged again. Manny was ready as he scrambled to his hands and knees. Moxie halted. Moxie faced a dangerous adversary here, one that could kill him. Moxie's crooked tail bushed out, and he hissed, showing fangs.

Manny got to his feet, cursing and wiping his bloody face. Manny swung his arm across a countertop sending spice bottles, and utensils flying. He sought something.

Cloudy paused at the slit in the door before running through. The noise behind her was deafening. Cloudy was witnessing something that totally went against her training. Moxie caught her gaze, and then renewed the attack when Manny turned his back on the cat. Moxie clawed into the back of Manny's balding head.

Cloudy mewed, asking Moxie to flee with her. Moxie hesitated, and Manny pulled the cat off his head. Manny tried to drop kick the tomcat, but lost his balance as his leg came up and his stationary foot slid on the spilled sauces on the floor. Manny crashed to the floor, and his face bounced off the corner of the prep table gashing his cheek. Manny saw it, his mighty meat cleaver! Manny picked it up and scrambled to his feet, and charged both cats.

The waitresses rushed through the double doors in time to see Manny hacking through the screen door with the meat cleaver.

"When I catch you, I'll skin you and make chow mien out of you!" Manny threw the cleaver after them, and it clanged against the *Dumpster* as both cats vanished into the night.

The last waitress on duty scolded Manny, "If we've told you once, perhaps more than a thousand times to get rid of that cat, and fix that screen door. Now look at you!"

She applied rubbing alcohol to his swelling scratches.

"You're a mess; I'm taking you to the emergency room."

Manny winced, but he rejected her. "No, there are still a few customers out there to be served. I can wait until we're closed."

"No one liked that evil thing but you. Now look at you! You'll probably need rabies shots or something worse. How did that ruckus get started anyway?"

Manny gently patted the diamond necklace in his pocket, and with a painful grin he said, "I must've stepped on his tail."

THE BLACK DUKE COULDN'T FIGHT his temptation any longer about Starlight. "Wise one, I'm lost. I hunger inside, a hunger so deep, and all-consuming that it might destroy me completely if I can't find a way to satisfy it."

"Many visions have come to me, strong one. I know; I see your desire. She's very near, and if you act swiftly, then she'll always be at your side. I know this. Your destinies are locked together, but beware for she is also your weakness. She may be the end of you."

Seldom Seen became very animated. He paced like a caged panther.

Wisecat continued, "Earlier today she sat here, seeking knowledge of you. Cloudy has much to learn if she's to survive on the streets. She needs you."

"Cloudy?" Seldom Seen knew she'd be different now, but her essence would be the basic her. He'd emotionally perish from regret unless he found Cloudy right away. Seldom Seen moved quickly to the hole in the roof. If Cloudy was near, then every minute counted against him.

Before he disappeared Wisecat spoke, "You must kill King Rat!"

A moment later, Wisecat was alone. Wisecat did all she could to set the wheel of fate rolling in a good direction for Seldom Seen. Wisecat hoped the big black tomcat would survive the inevitable conflict that was destined to be. Wisecat sat in the noon Sun's warmth. A blind cat can see no evil acts, but she felt the ugliness of King Rat's reign erupting to spread plague, and death on the earth.

Tutulem silently backtracked, and disappeared from sight. In just a few moments he had become extremely valuable.

Moxie and Cloudy ran until they reached a place where he felt safe. Still full of the fighting spirit; he playfully cuffed Cloudy's big head. Moxie darted, and feinted; trying to get her to play. Once Cloudy realized it was just roughhousing; she enjoyed the mock combat.

Respect soon replaced her fear of the young Duke. A devil don't care attitude made Moxie a dangerous force to cross swords against. If there was a fight between tomcats, Cloudy knew he'd be one of the two involved. Cloudy saw it in his eyes when she summoned him to flee, but Moxie chose to continue the battle against overwhelming odds.

Cloudy stumbled across the lifestyle she'd been looking for in Moxie's hardcore nature. He was a juvenile, and rough, but perhaps some of her aristocratic style would rub off on him. It was worth a try.

They fought mock battles, rolling across the turf. Her swift paw strokes managed to find their mark as well. In her earlier lifestyle, none of that would've been possible. During cat shows, all she could do was stare through her cage longingly, teasing her royal counterparts with her flirtatious ways, leaving them flustered by their inability to get at her. Suddenly, playing with a male's emotions had interesting consequences.

Moxie stumbled onto something special too, but he lost a prized feeding spot to protect her from Manny. He'd have to start hunting mice again.

Moxie paused as his attitude changed. He looked about while flexing his whiskers. Cloudy cuffed him with a fleeting stroke. Moxie ignored her, and thought about the hunger they'd be feeling this evening. There were always mice to be caught on the streets, and in the fields, but he was no longer certain of their traveling patterns. It'd been months since he caught one of the tasteless rodents. His acquired tastes for Manny's spicy cooking was over. Moxie looked at Cloudy lying in the grass so content, and relaxed. She was too tame. Moxie surmised she must've been raised in a house her entire lifestyle. She'd have trouble hunting tonight.

"When the Sun goes down the mice will come out, and that's when we'll begin our hunt. Stick with me, and you'll be able to catch mice too."

Cloudy moved close enough so their whiskers touched. Their eyes lit with the flame of passion. Moxie bit into the back of her neck, and applied himself.

Seldom Seen deeply regretted the macho attitude he displayed to thwart Cloudy's seductive come-on. Cloudy lured him to the screen door innocently enough, and then awed him with a soft purr; and a press against the barrier with a wanting which was unmistakable lust. The way Cloudy licked her mouth, and her incessant stare made him feel important; and Seldom Seen relived those moments repeatedly.

She was hot, and in heat.

Seldom Seen fantasized himself into an unparalleled love. He thought about what Cloudy was, her large head, and luxurious coat made her exotic; but she was more than that.

Seldom Seen only ate a few crickets that constantly announced themselves during the night, for water he had a few licks of a muddy puddle. That was all the hunting savvy mustered since his first encounter with Starlight.

Seldom Seen went along the sidewalk, and then crossed the street keeping a wary eye out for danger. He watched for snooping canines, speeding cars, and adolescent humans who might do him harm. He finally settled behind the curbside tire of a parked car.

It had been nice to communicate with her telepathically. Only in excitement or warning did felines vocalize. It was enough to look into each other's eyes to understand detailed thoughts.

The eerie vibrating noise of the cicadas in the trees drilled into his head like an alarm going off. It peaked, and then quickly faded. Seldom Seen bolted from under the car, and jumped a fence blocking his path. He didn't know where to go, but Seldom Seen had to find Cloudy fast.

Dusk fell over the treetops announcing the beginning of the second half of the day. Moxie prepared for the evening with some deep stretches. Tonight, he'd summon rusty instincts for the hunt.

Cloudy woke when Moxie stirred. Rousing play and exploring had been their lot for the day. The nap took them to early evening. Cloudy was hungry.

She was afraid to roam freely in the midnight. The wide-open vastness overhead always shattered her confidence. She had been an indoor cat, painted ceilings comforted Cloudy with a sense of security, but with such a young brute at her side now, she knew it was safe to venture forth into blackness, and challenge anything it held.

Moxie chose to hunt in the ghetto streets tonight; not having to push through tall grass, and bushes would save energy and widen their hunting radius, plus the ghetto maintained a large rodent population. As Moxie moved into the night his senses were attuned to every living thing in range. Some sounds he tuned out, others he zeroed in on. The only real dangers were cars; sudden bright lights bearing down sent a bolt of panic into the most seasoned stray. It took only a second to be struck down while deciding which way to run, those cars were very fast.

Cloudy's presence disappeared as Moxie concentrated on the hunt. Moxie wouldn't teach Cloudy directly. She'd have to learn by watching how he did it. They roamed lighted streets, and like thieves they violated the night.

Seldom Seen felt the once absent strength surge through him, and electrify his being. Cloudy was near. His feline senses felt her. The lust for the hunt was back. Seldom Seen's whiskers were perky, and his wide eyes more alive from excitement. He leaped onto a fence, and walked along it easily. The Sun surrendered to the night, and the new Moon would make him almost invisible, like a shadow overlapping another shadow.

Seldom Seen looked up, and paused. Thousands of stars splashed over the blackness of deep space, illuminating the depths of infinity. Some of those stars were millions of light years away. One star's light had caught his attention though, reflecting into his imagination with the warmth of a profound love.

Cloudy noticed Moxie's serious change; and the lithe strength of his tuned muscles as he crept from one position to another seeking prey. She watched the young master. Moxie's eyes caught hers for a moment, and she saw the concentration of a seasoned killer.

Moxie heard a noise, and slumped into a compact form on the ground. All senses focused forward. His body moved over the ground like water, seeping into every crack, and crevice that offered space. Moxie zeroed in on the rustle behind the garbage cans. He took in a long breath, and moved stealthily towards that sound. Cloudy froze.

Suddenly Moxie darted behind the garbage cans, and disappeared; thudding paw strokes found the target. Cloudy darted into the tight space in time to see him chewing on the head of a wiggling mouse. It had never been that easy for Cloudy, but she was willing to try again. Cloudy crept off with new confidence. The hunt was on.

As they moved into the open, and under a street lamp, Cloudy realized the reflected sparkling from the diamond necklace was gone. She thought about that for a moment. Without Moxie, it would probably still be there. The kinship she felt with Tink immediately dissolved. Cloudy was another level above the garbage-foraging alley cat now. Cloudy had the potential of a hunting stray cat, something to be feared as lethal. Cloudy now dignified herself as a part of the upper crust of street life; and she owed it all to Moxie.

Cloudy moved towards Moxie to bestow her loving warmth. Moxie arched his back, caught off guard. Before Cloudy could react Moxie attacked her with a paw strike. Cloudy went sprawling backwards onto the tar. Once down, his claws raked Cloudy's tender stomach as she tried to escape.

Cloudy froze, feeling the sting of deep scratches. She was injured! Moxie was on top, and ready to dish out more punishment if necessary to protect his catch. The taste of blood sent him over the edge. Moxie cherished real battles where a serious adversary made a match for him. Cloudy was not a threat. He eased away, and swallowed the rodent's tail.

Cloudy righted herself. Afraid to run off; she waited to see what would happen. There was a period of tense silence, and Cloudy refused to run away to tend her wounds, and admit defeat. As Starlight, she'd been a perfect cat; but as Cloudy, she'd be permanently scarred.

"Never approach while I'm eating."

Moxie flicked his broken tail, "You'll live, be almost as good as new in a few weeks. Let's go."

Smarting with pain, Cloudy obediently followed. On the pavement were a few drops of blood, marking her first defeat.

Seldom Seen caterwauled to the night trying to release his frustrations, and it was a haunting sound. He leaped down, and rushed towards a destination he didn't know yet, feeling Cloudy's presence, Seldom Seen ran with his heart ready to burst with desire. Restless energy filled him. The fumes of memories drove him onward.

Seldom Seen could feel Cloudy, and he charged forward; not waiting for the moment when they'd meet again, but aggressively pursuing it. His imagination blended visions of the past with the anticipation, and glory of a future lifestyle with her.

Moxie paused as the echo of another tomcat resounded within his turf. He eased past Cloudy, and turned towards that sound. Something was happening that he couldn't tolerate; another tomcat on his turf.

Cloudy felt more excitement waiting to be unleashed just beyond her senses. Moxie felt it too, and he became restless. They ran together; Cloudy looked up at the night sky. Millions of stars showed Heaven's infinity, but they also stood as the gate that stopped the mind's penetration into black space. Her imagination sought to go beyond that barrier, and venture into the realm of the psychic. Cloudy knew Seldom Seen was coming.

Moxie stopped, and looked around with Cloudy at his side. He felt the hair-thin trigger of aggression squeeze him like never before. The black tomcat materialized out of the darkness. Moxie's back arched, and he hissed with anger.

Seldom Seen had arrived!

Seldom Seen attacked, but Moxie met him more than halfway. They struck heavily into each other, and crashed to the ground entwined in tooth and claw.

Moxie drew first blood. Crimson dripped from Seldom Seen's back, and shoulder as they separated. Seldom Seen attacked again glimpsing Cloudy as he went after Moxie with a barrage of paw swipes. Cloudy sat calmly as one who expected such displays of emotion.

Cloudy realized she was something special. She felt more powerful now than any victory in a cat show, out here on the streets it was a life or death struggle, and she was a prize to be cherished.

This new awareness took firm hold of Cloudy as she watched this great duel over her as a possession. She had pleaded with Seldom Seen to stay with her, but now Cloudy sat calmly to see if he was good enough to be her champion.

Seldom Seen fought the great calico. The Duke of Tewksbury, first quadrant was a legend on the streets for being so young, ruthless, and successful. Seldom Seen remembered Moxie, a tri-colored tomcat who had defeated him many times when he tried to take Manny's place as his turf. After those defeats Seldom Seen went off to forge a smaller empire away from Moxie. Seldom Seen never wanted to face that cat again in combat but now; he went after Moxie with new determination. Seldom Seen's quest for Cloudy had brought him new courage to face Moxie again.

Seldom Seen rarely went hungry, and managed to find live prey, or got a cheap bite from rubbish. The meal Marlene gave was his only real nourishment in the past few days. His reservoir of strength wasn't fully energized for such an awesome tomcat.

Moxie was the younger of the two cats. He pressed against Seldom Seen like an evil storm. His paws struck with the quickness of lightning bolts, and his hiss boomed like thunder. Seldom Seen gave no ground, and countered with a timed paw strike to the nose as Moxie pressured him with another strong charge.

Moxie recoiled, hurt! Moxie thought he could quickly overpower the older cat, but quickly checked the bold tactic as blood spouted from a deep slice that almost halved his tiny pink nose. The taste of his own blood spurred him on to crush Seldom Seen right away.

It was like a dream to Cloudy. At times, Moxie seemed to fight nothing at all as Seldom Seen's black coat blended with the moonless night. Only the gleam of bared fangs, and wide eyes made Seldom Seen visible to her.

Ears back, Moxie charged again, tangling with Seldom Seen in a ball of fast fury. Moxie believed he was the toughest, and refused to be defeated. They battled, trying to strike the one sudden blow that meant the downfall for the other. The rules were simple, the first one who fled was vanquished, and the winner took Cloudy as the prize.

Cloudy was mesmerized. No ritzy cat ever fought for her affections. Marlene always picked Cloudy's mates to obtain the optimum breeding for the expensive Persian pedigree.

Cloudy was truly impressed by the two Dukes, and their determination to win her. She admired both, but Seldom Seen possessed a sensuality that attracted her. He always seemed to come out of the night on the crest of a spectacular entrance. Seldom Seen also had the sleek lines of some of the pedigrees Cloudy faced in competition, more than that; he had the street savvy that made his lifestyle so appealing to her.

Moxie was ruthless in the attack; his whole chest ran red because of the injury to his nose. They tangled, and separated over and over, and it was turning into an endurance match after the opening swift attacks. Moxie knew what Seldom Seen wanted, and he'd never surrender such a valuable prize. Moxie's breath came in gasps as the blood congealed in his nostrils. Again Moxie tried for a quick devastating victory with another mad rush, but Seldom Seen was much too wary, and the black cat gave ground until Moxie was exhausted and had to pause. During this break Seldom Seen stole a glance at Cloudy. She caught his gaze with unemotional detachment.

At that very moment Moxie charged with a powerful paw strike sending Seldom Seen sprawling backwards. Moxie was spent, but that paw strike hurt Seldom Seen. Moxie renewed the attack sensing victory. Seldom Seen lost his sharp edge, and began to die an emotional death, because Cloudy sat a few meters away, just patiently waiting for whoever would win her.

How could Cloudy cheapen herself in such a way when she belonged with him! All his fancy visions about himself, and her shattered as Moxie once again started to take him down.

Cloudy seethed with the predicament the two Dukes forced on her. She was to be won or lost, and with no say in the consequences! Seldom Seen landed on his back from the paw strike, and Moxie was thrashing him. There wasn't time to retaliate, because Moxie had been too quick. Moxie's fangs locked on Seldom Seen's windpipe choking the black cat.

Seldom Seen felt the needle-tipped fangs go into his neck, and then his breath stopped.

Cloudy lunged, and hit Moxie from behind clawing his back like a savage beast. Moxie bolted away from the surprise attack unaware of the identity of the new adversary. Moxie reacted instinctively, and vanished, fearing a dog had come across the battle. Moxie leaped the nearest fence and disappeared into the night.

Seldom Seen righted himself, and faced Cloudy. Victory was snatched from certain death, and it was her doing. Blood trickled from his gashed shoulder.

"Oh, you're wounded!" Cloudy examined his gash. Cloudy had saved his life. Cloudy sat in front of him, and tended her own wounds.

After days of turmoil, Seldom Seen was at peace with himself, and calmness floated into him. Seldom Seen gazed into her soft eyes.

After tending to their injuries, Seldom Seen led Cloudy to another place, to his own turf, and there the night was long.

Wisecat

TUTULEM HOPPED, AND SCURRIED THROUGH the mounds of garbage. The city dump had never been his home, but he knew it well. Houses were more to his taste, especially in the winter.

The dump was the world of the dregs; rats, mice, opossums, and raccoons flourished there. Poison bait set by humans took their toll, but all species survived.

Tutulem favored the warm and docile environment of the humans. Only something of importance would bring him to the dump at this late hour. His trek had been long and dangerous to reach the outskirts of town. A hunting stray cat would make a quick meal of him, but he made it.

He located the wreck, a rusted out sedan. It would've been a vintage car if it still ran. It rested solidly on a hill of trash that was bulldozed several feet high. The landmark had been dubbed the Palace, but it also stood as King Rat's fortress. Most of the windows were intact, but years of dirt made them opaque.

Tutulem climbed the mound, and entered through the missing door on the driver's side. He moved towards the rear seats and into the trunk compartment through a hole chewed to provide access into the throne room. Dim rays of light filtered through the rusting lid of the trunk when the Sun or Moon shone, dropping dozens of thin beams into the large chamber to illuminate it. Paper trash was shredded to soften the cold hardness of the steel compartment.

King Rat was in the middle of the trunk, exhausted after tending to a new batch of female rats. The ones already pregnant rested in a corner counting their days. Many more tried to rouse the King to action. Tutulem climbed over them to get King Rat's attention.

Tutulem detailed all he heard and saw. King Rat squeaked with glee. He didn't know where the black cat was now, but sooner or later the cat would return to the boarded up house. What interested King Rat even more was the plot Wisecat was spinning.

Tutulem led King Rat into the ghetto where the abandoned house stood. As they moved from the wilderness they went underground through the sewer system. Along the way, other rats made the trek with them.

Wisecat roused from a troubled sleep. A disturbing vision came in the night of a world overrun by super rats, pillaging and spreading disease everywhere, it was the Age of the Rat. Wisecat also saw a dead and butchered Siamese cat; it was she, her maggot infested body decomposing to bones and fur with Seldom Seen nowhere to be found.

Noise echoed into the vast attic now, increasing one hundred fold every second as the pattering of thousands of feet came from everywhere. Wisecat licked one paw and waited. Her old yellow and brittle claws would be little use in this type of battle, one against thousands.

Unafraid, King Rat took up a position beside the old Siamese, and that gave him an air of invincibility as hundreds of rodents filed into the attic and enveloped the pair with a hunger for blood. King Rat looked over his audience and wouldn't disappoint them.

Hundreds of rats, and more than that number tenfold in mice rimmed the edges of the burned opening in the roof to witness King Rat's wrath. Some fell into the masses below when they were pushed over the edge by others who wanted to see.

King Rat spoke, "Here is the criminal mastermind who plotted to assassinate me!

"For millennia, our kind has waited for the days which are almost here! In less than one rising of the Moon my handiwork will be done to start the beginning of the Age of the Rat! I'm the action from which ever-expanding waves will develop and recapture our lost beginnings. I will deliver you from darkness, and you will walk in the sunlight, smell fresh scents instead of rotten garbage!"

It was the same speech drilled into the psyche of the rodents, but this time King Rat would give the sermon, and sacrifice this old cat.

"I will deliver all of your enemies to you, and most treacherous of all; the humans! We are the true survivors from long ago. We were here first and let nothing dare stand against me!"

Wisecat decided not to defend herself, not even with words. Instead, she reached Seldom Seen psychically to warn him of the dangers ahead. *"Be brave my friend. My time here has come to an end, and I must leave you. Your life is about to go into the fire, but you're strong enough to survive. Destroy this fiend where he breeds. Bring death to him, and to those born from him."*

King Rat squeaked, "This old cat, and the black cat plotted to destroy your dreams; the Age of the Rat.

"They plotted to kill me! I'm wise, and we the many are too strong. They were found out! She must die!"

King Rat was the judge and executioner; the sentence is death. A crescendo of squeaks went up.

King Rat's long chisel teeth sank into the Wisecat's neck, it was an ugly kiss as his hulking form enveloped her like a great vampire, and his weight easily pulled her down. He gnawed halfway through her neck before she died.

ONE WEEK PASSED AFTER MOXIE's defeat. The brief affair with Cloudy sent his fortunes tumbling into a dramatic fall. Moxie's tasty meals from the restaurant were gone. If he entertained the foolish thought of going back, he'd be killed. Foraging in garbage cans led to his nose becoming infected. It swelled with infection, and dried blood making it hard to breathe. Moxie couldn't hunt mice without quickly exhausting himself.

Moxie's tongue licked out over his ailing nose making him wince. His life had never been this poor. All Moxie had accomplished vanished in the wink of an eye. The worst hurt though was to his big ego. Moxie finally concluded that Cloudy betrayed him, and turned victory to Seldom Seen. Her treachery was responsible for Moxie's defeat! He planned to win Cloudy back, and then teach her a memorable lesson for the betrayal.

Moxie arched his back to stretch and his healing scabs cracked and opened new places from which blood seeped out. Moxie ignored the pain and went off to find something to eat. He came out of a group of hedges and moved onto the street.

Seldom Seen awoke feeling fresh. His love for Cloudy blossomed like a rose opening for the first time on a spring day. Within one week Cloudy became the center of his universe. His obsession turned into love, the most powerful love he'd known.

His tongue caressed Cloudy's head affectionately. Seldom Seen had been strong enough to channel his desire into one goal and reap the reward, but he wasn't content with his newly won situation. As Cloudy lay beside him, Seldom Seen realized he couldn't relax. His life with Cloudy was just beginning and he must reinforce his presence a thousand fold. He didn't want to be a passing fad, something to toss away when amusement was spent. Seldom Seen saw winning was just the preliminary, close up though she'd scrutinize their day-to-day relationship, and then judge him from that.

Cloudy woke with a mellow purr. With Moxie, she felt like a tortured prisoner. Moxie's presence was like a heavy iron collar of domination around her being. With Seldom Seen, her soul emotions blew as freely as the wind without boundaries. When obstacles arose her emotions reformed from the turbulence, and still moved upward with the anticipation of new goals. The breath of deep love was in her too!

During the past few days, Cloudy learned much about the mysterious tomcat. He'd been raised like herself, in a household, but misfortune forced its hand early in Seldom Seen's life.

The house fire that changed his lifestyle came in the still of the night when everyone was asleep. He was the first to know and he'd always remember the horror, the screaming and the choking smoke.

Cocoa ran trying to find a safe place. Sirens and breaking glass only added to the confusion. A pair of strong hands scooped him up, and tossed him through a broken window to safety.

He watched his home begin to burn through the roof. People came to watch. It was a desperate race to save the house from total destruction.

Cocoa was just a small kitten, one month after being weaned from his mother. He watched the smoke and embers spiral into the night sky. He felt a sense of romance about the night, and its starry lights. That was the first time he saw the sky. As the kitten looked up he never felt smaller, and then realized he was part of the whole, and the feeling was impressive. He wanted to feel the night's mysterious aura and be a part of it. He wondered away from the destruction of his home, and embraced the solitude of a warm summer's eve.

His baptism of fire into the streets began that very night. Hunger pangs days later made him realize it was a unforgiving environment, and that food wasn't served up at regular intervals. He wandered a long a way, but then his determination to survive gave out.

A Siamese cat leaped down from a high place like an angel. It was a young Wisecat. She'd been observing the kitten's predicament for a few days, and she decided to go to his rescue. Wisecat carried the tiny orphan in her mouth. He was too small to get into any garbage cans. When the kitten crumpled, Wisecat moved to rescue him.

As the months grew into years Seldom Seen became attuned to Wisecat's ways. His hunting skills became legendary. Quick wits and a strong young body gave Seldom Seen what he needed for nightlong forays of hunting with Wisecat. They were relentless, the elite hunters. When the night came, Seldom Seen was less substantial than a shadow in the night. Moonless nights were his best hunts. The young cat never failed to fill his stomach on the pitch-black nights.

In the beginning they worked together, but as Wisecat's vision dimmed with age, she became more stationary. Wisecat's days seemed longer, and more uneventful as she became a prisoner to blindness, and during long spells alone she began to look within. That's when her psychic powers manifested into clear visions of what would come. Yes, where Wisecat's physical sight failed, another kind took over. Without having to worry about food, Wisecat focused her entire awareness towards this new ability and mastered it.

Seldom Seen found himself hunting for two, but he didn't mind because it was the price to pay for gaining a new lifestyle. Wisecat was there when he needed help, and he would never fail her.

Wisecat made him more than a survivor; she had molded a master for the hunt. Seldom Seen went where few strays go to catch extra booty, the city dump.

King Rat

SEA GULLS GLIDED ON THE morning thermals in circular patterns above the city dump. Some dived, and rose again, spurring one another on with graceful acrobatics. Below, among the mountains of trash where King Rat lived, it was a time to rejoice, and a time to die. Several litters were born during the hot summer night and fifty-seven baby rats curled respectfully around their mothers. Some were much larger than their siblings.

King Rat moved among them, his pink eye sentencing to death those not born with his super genes. He immediately destroyed the normal ones, leaving bloody clumps in each brood as he went on to the next batch. King Rat learned from the genetic scientist, no nourishment would be wasted on those who didn't fit into his master plan. When he was done, eleven baby rats still lived. That was the beginning; it was the dawn of the Age of the Rat.

King Rat came a long way since his escape from the labs. Seeing Julia murdering his brothers, and sisters with massive doses of poison meant his end was near. When King Rat bit the tip of her finger off months ago she'd promised to make his suffering great. King Rat's usefulness as a lab rat was over. In desperation he forced his way out of his cage with pure strength. King Rat found a chipped cinder block in the wall, and with determination he gnawed straight through to the outer corridor. Feeling naked in the stark light he scurried along the wall seeking cover, an opened door provided King Rat's means of escape. The stairway went down to the main entrance. King Rat slunk along walls, and furnishings. He managed to elude the stationary guard watching a professional baseball game on his portable set. When King Rat's hulking form tripped the electric eye; the security guard didn't notice. The glass doors slid open on their rails, and King Rat was free.

King Rat inhaled nature's fresh scents, and he liked it. King Rat took in another deep breath and realized his great accomplishment. In one desperate stroke, a super rat became the master of his dreams, and soon the keeper of other's destinies.

When humans rose to the top rank in nature, the rodents were sentenced, and banished to the outskirts of what Man conquered. Man's alliance with cats drove the rodents from Man's warm caves, and then his huts, and finally his houses. Rats were treated scornfully, something to be trapped, and killed wherever they intruded into Man's lifestyle.

Wherever Man disposed his trash became the safest places for the rodents to multiply and survive. Those were the places Man shunned, and every day the dumps in every town, were growing. Man's population expanded, and his amount of trash increased.

The rodent's domain quickly solidified beside Man's fabricated world. City dumps became places where they could breed and live, but the humans were very persistent in ways to destroy them. Rodents survived through determination, and a desire to live. They refused to be exterminated the way Man had wiped out other species. The carrier pigeon, and the dodo bird would never rise again, while other species teetered on the brink of extinction.

The city dump in which King Rat lived was high above the town of Taverny, a rustic place where business people escaped the bustle of city life fifty miles away. The town had been established to accommodate the influx of commuters who worked in the metropolis.

This dump overlooked the houses, and crisscrossed streets far below. Down there was a place where King Rat and his kind couldn't move about during the daylight. Only during the night could he sneak into the places where the twinkling streetlights shined. He made moves to change all that.

On the far side of the dump, untamed acres of flowers and uncut grass spread to the horizon, and it was a place where Man would eventually conquer, but for the moment it was the home of many creatures. Those acres had never felt the touch of civilization, and the open fields were a paradise to those who lived there.

Those fields and the forest beyond were a part of Seldom Seen's hunting turf. At midnight he stalked there. In midday, he frolicked, chasing butterflies and honeybees. He savored the fresh, flavorful scents of the flowers, and the spongy turf under his paws as opposed to the concrete and tar of the suburbs. The rustling sounds the wind made as it whipped through the fields of long grass sent him on running sprees in an attempt to catch its invisible form.

When he wanted to relax, and forget everything human, then cattails waved overhead and hid the blue sky. The sounds of dried twigs, and straw crackled under his soft pads. Stems of growth pressed against his flanks raining seeds that stuck to his coat, only to be spread elsewhere. He was one with nature, and enveloped in her touch. He couldn't convey those feelings about it to Cloudy; it would be something she'd have to experience herself.

That terrain kept him in tune with freedom. He got lost out there often, sometimes for days, and being away from everything that was familiar was scary, but Seldom Seen was stronger because of it. He was liberated, and could roam anywhere he pleased; getting lost sometimes was the price one paid for that freedom.

Starlight

MARLENE SPENT EVERY DAY SEARCHING for Starlight. Most of the time was spent driving in circles through neighboring towns, hoping to see her lost Persian.

Each day, Marlene's search area expanded. Ads in all the local papers proved fruitless. At night, she prayed for her cat's safety and quick return. During the day and evening she set out a fresh plate of tuna or mackerel on the doorstep hoping to draw nearby felines. It hadn't worked so far to lure her back, but it was still a chance. Starlight refused to be found!

Marlene retired from secretarial work when her hobby of breeding Persians proved more lucrative. Marlene's wealth also came from her grandfather's business dealings and her deceased husband's ownership of five businesses during his rise in the Tavenry community, which she sold.

Marlene's pedigree of Persians had a worldwide reputation and she'd won the highest awards with Starlight, which reflected the expertise in her breeding skills. Starlight had successfully defended her ribbon for three continuous years.

Before Starlight's ascension, Nova, her mother was queen for five straight years. Nova was buried in a plot in the largest garden bed along the front path to the main entrance of the house. Marlene kept Nova's presence alive with photographs, ribbons and newspaper clippings.

A woman of seventy-one, Marlene was still bright and agile with a wiry physique. She adopted a few of the Persian's habits over the years. Stretching each morning kept her joints and muscles lithe and firm like those of her cats. Being inquisitive like them kept her mind alert as she explored some of life's deepest mysteries.

Starlight had just entered a breeding cycle and she was being matched up with a superb champion Persian from England. His owner was shipping him personally for optimum results and a lot of money hung in the balance if Cloudy wasn't recovered immediately.

Starlight certainly meant more to Marlene than just money; Starlight filled her idle days with love and caring. Without Starlight, Marlene's nights became hollow and stale. Her evening ritual of reading newspaper clippings relaxed her into a comfortable night's sleep, but now she couldn't bare the thoughts of what could be happening to her cat.

Marlene turned off the night lamp, and pulled the sheets snugly around her neck. It promised to be another night of restless slumber.

A scent came to Moxie; it was the aroma of fresh fish. Moxie stepped up to the picket fence, his whiskers flaring in excitement. Moxie leaped the barrier and cautiously sought out the base for the fishy aroma. He didn't like to enter fenced areas but he might have found a new place to dine. Moxie was willing to risk it. Perhaps his luck was changing.

Moxie saw another tomcat feasting at the bowl. He drove the stray away with a hiss, and some cutting paw strokes. Moxie bit into the fish. It'd been a long time since he ate anything fresh. He purred like a contented king. The cloak of poverty was falling away.

Moxie licked the bowl clean, and then surveyed his new turf. The huge yard was encased by a picket fence and dotted by shrubbery. He stretched his scarred back and relaxed on the doorstep, someone had to live here.

Marlene peeked through her bedroom window. She heard the fight on her doorstep and knew it was probably tomcats but she had to make sure it wasn't Starlight come home. When she witnessed the two tomcats fighting, a teardrop coursed down her cheek and new hair-thin wrinkles seemed to develop on her face at that very moment. Marlene fell backwards onto her bed.

Cloudy quickly changed. Cloudy became more alert to her surroundings, a curious cat that investigated everything. Nothing was taken for granted anymore. A new world opened up for her; becoming more real than the fantasies Cloudy wove during her days in the Tavenry.

If Cloudy was to survive on the streets then nocturnal hunting had to become her primary occupation. Once she'd been a feline of just the daylight hours where she used that time for leisure, and then slept all night.

Now catnaps became the norm. Hunting was a twenty-four-hour-a-day job and Cloudy slept when she could, preferably when she wasn't hungry. With Seldom Seen leading the way, her rugged path to freedom became smoother. Her physique hardened from the disciplined exertion applied from street survival. Outwardly, Cloudy was stronger and more agile, but she still hadn't snared a field mouse. With his mastery of hunting, Seldom Seen caught extra mice for her.

Foraging in garbage cans proved profitless one day.

"I'm hungry Seldom Seen."

Seldom Seen smiled mentally. Nothing motivated more than a growling stomach. Seldom Seen purposely took Cloudy to the worst spots to rummage for cheap bites of food. Seldom Seen wanted her very hungry for the evening's prowl. He paused as Cloudy came close. Seldom Seen liked the feel of her soft and plentiful coat against him. The pressure Cloudy applied as she rubbed along his flanks was a very transparent attempt to get a free meal from him. He wouldn't be coerced into satisfying her appetite this time. It was time to teach Cloudy the tactics of hunting.

They set out.

They found a stretch of cattails and sleeping flowers. Their plan was elementary, and they entered the field from opposite ends. They would drive fleeing mice into each other's killing zone. It couldn't fail.

Cloudy moved through the thick foliage. She looked up at the night sky barely visible beyond the growth that overlapped her head. Frogs and insects added a strange orchestra, a very different type of sound than the birds during the daylight. Cloudy noted those differences. Every few feet a lightening beetle flashed.

They moved towards each other. Ahead of Cloudy, field mice fled. She remembered not to chase them, only the ones that came towards her. Both cats made deliberate efforts to make their positions known to the rodents, and that made the mice panic.

Cloudy's moment had arrived. A mouse was running right towards her fleeing Seldom Seen's disquieting rumble through the brush. Her keen vision saw the rodent's movements against the still grasses. Cloudy lunged and pinned it against the turf. With the mouse firmly in her needle tipped claws, she broke its neck, and bit off its head. Another mouse almost got past her as she relished her victory, but she caught it with a pounce and a smack of her paw.

The mice dangled from her jaws by their tails like extended yo-yos. Seldom Seen appeared through the brush to face her with two mice and a frog. They sat and devoured their meals, which satisfied the hunger in their stomachs. Once their meals were consumed they rolled and frolicked in the cattails in a victory celebration. They wouldn't catch any more mice this evening. Inside the circle of matted turf, and walls of tall cattails they relaxed in each other's comfort. It felt good to be alive and free, fighting and winning in nature's battle for survival; being with the one you loved, and being loved back.

Seldom Seen rested on Cloudy's plentiful coat. Overhead, towering stalks gave way to black heavens. His love was deeper than the space above. A meteoroid blazed across the sky, turning colors before burning out with a shower of sparks. Suddenly, he realized that Wisecat was starving without the meals he always gave her. He'd been so involved with love that he forgot about Wisecat.

Sᴇʟᴅᴏᴍ Sᴇᴇɴ ᴡᴏᴋᴇ ᴀɴᴅ sᴛʀᴇᴛᴄʜᴇᴅ to the tune of singing birds and the rustle of soft breezes blowing through the bush. The Sun was still below the horizon. Seldom Seen gathered up his thoughts, last night had been a big success.

Since Seldom Seen teamed up with Cloudy his nightmares had stopped too. He no longer dreaded the lifestyle, or fear what would become of him in the end. It seemed as if new energy carried Seldom Seen effortlessly through his days and nights. Seldom Seen would show Cloudy everything he knew and they'd grow together. He gazed at Cloudy, cherishing every second they were together. Cloudy slept for a moment longer, and then stirred as she felt the presence of his eyes.

Seldom Seen licked the gash he got during his fight with Moxie to win her. It healed, but it was still tender to the touch. He thought of the scars Cloudy had from Moxie. If Seldom Seen and Moxie ever crossed paths again, he'd kill Moxie.

Cloudy stretched and tuned her body for a new day. Things got a lot better for her since teaming with Seldom Seen. New confidence surged through her after the previous night's events. Cloudy began to believe that she could survive on the streets. Cloudy wanted to tell Tink about her success.

"Seldom Seen, you were right. This lifestyle isn't for all felines. Many of my old acquaintances would perish under the Sun, and Moon. They definitely wouldn't approve of my current situation, but they're there and we're here. Let's live life as best we can."

Seldom Seen reflected upon her words and could think of nothing more to add. They went off to the suburbs for something to eat.

Foraging in garbage cans was always the first order of business each morning. That's when everything was quiet and the garbage had just been put out, so there was the promise of something to eat. It was a lazy way to get bites, but all stray cats did it, and it saved valuable energy for the demanding hunts at night when the mice came out.

Every morning, Tink was the first to explore the new day's trash. The cat that couldn't be stealthy tinkled her way down the sidewalk. She pushed aside a half-cocked lid on a can and peeked in.

Tink led the most solitary life of all the alley cats. The other strays knew of her, but Tink was known as the cat that couldn't catch a bloody meal. They shunned Tink worried that her bad luck might rub off onto them.

It was rumored that Bastet was punishing her for some misdeed in a previous lifestyle, but Tink fled her master because of savage beatings. Better her current lifestyle than being dead or crippled, but rumors flourished about Tink like weeds in an unkempt garden.

The new rumor was how Tink butchered her own newborns to be rid of them to surf the garbage at her whim, the only true love she surrendered for.

Tink no longer cared to fight the rumors, which made the rumors, appear true. They all doomed Tink from her first days on the streets, but she managed to outlive some of her worst antagonists. Tink simply played the hand she was dealt.

After consuming a few leftover tidbits, Tink licked her chops and leaped from the receptacle with a tinkle. After cleaning her coat, Tink pondered where else to go. When she looked up, she saw Cloudy and Seldom Seen coming out of some shrubs and into the open.

Cloudy quickly closed the distance between them to face the tabby, while Seldom Seen moved with a slow, measured pace. Cloudy pawed Tink's tin bells, "You're not so hard to find. How have you been?"

Tink glanced at Seldom Seen as he poked in the garbage can she just vacated. Another smack at her bells made Tink look at Cloudy again. "Good as good can be. My stomach's full, and it's a sunny morning. How have you been Seldom Seen?"

Seldom Seen buried his head in a Chinese fast-food container to get at a few shreds of chicken mixed with the rice and vegetables.

Seldom Seen leaped from the first garbage can and chose another to investigate, leaning his forepaws on the edge to peer inside. A moment later, he jumped in for a better look.

Tink turned her attention to Cloudy. "I see you found him."

Cloudy went to the garbage can Seldom Seen was in and sat to groom her chest with a few licks. "Correction, he found me!"

Tink mewed, "There's nothing left Seldom Seen. You'll have to get up earlier than this to beat me!"

Cloudy went to Tink again and made her bells ring. "I have fantastic news! I got my first mouse last night! Mice will never escape me again!" Cloudy's eyes were filled with enthusiasm.

"It's so easy, Tink." Cloudy imitated her killing stroke, and hit the bells again.

"If I can do it, then you can too."

Seldom Seen popped his head up. "Don't make it sound so easy. Tink is cursed!"

Tink scratched at a flea, which made her bells sound, and then moved to the next set of cans farther up the block. Cloudy's enthusiasm swelled as she caught up to Tink. "Those bells are only your excuse! You're just a lazy cat. You need to try harder instead of giving in so easily to your weaknesses."

Tink was angry. "Don't be stupid! All is quiet at night! How can I sneak up on mice with this curse?"

"No, no, no, many creatures stir in the night. I've heard the racket. You don't make any more noise than they do, if you're careful."

Tink thought about that. "One lucky night and you think mice will die from your gaze. It isn't that easy honey. I've tried too many times, so many times that I've given up trying. Seldom Seen is right."

Tink looked at the black cat, "I am cursed, and I hate you for saying that about me! You were the only one who truly believed in me!"

Seldom Seen leaped to the sidewalk. There were no bites here. Tink had been thorough. He went in the opposite direction to get away from Tink. Cloudy moved away to follow him.

"You're just lazy!" Cloudy's feline eyes pleaded again.

"Give it another try young lady. If your will is strong enough then you can overcome anything. Look what I've accomplished. Give it another try and you'll be a winner too, but you mustn't stop trying!"

Tink watched them wander off in search for bites. She scratched at another flea with a hind leg, her bells rang loudly. Cloudy's words hurt her, as did her pleading eyes. She wondered if those eyes swayed Seldom Seen too. They disappeared through a hedge leaving Tink to wonder if there was any truth in what Cloudy said.

Tink realized she was in a bottomless pit of despair. She gave up the thought of snaring mice years ago. Cloudy was just a neophyte. Tink had been on the streets for years and she knew them as well as any stray, or alley cat. If Cloudy could do it, then she was determined to break the shackles of her poverty and rise above it.

"I like her." Cloudy said.

"Tink was the first stray I met after I escaped." She looked at Seldom Seen.

"She tried to help me find you when I was lost!"

It was true, Tink was the first stray Cloudy met. They had an unusual affinity for one another and that was something Seldom Seen would never understand.

Although Tink felt jealous of Cloudy, she was attracted to her elegance and high breeding style. Tink never met a feline like her, and probably never would again. She hoped some of Cloudy's good fortune would rub on her with the thoughts traded between them.

Cloudy

MOXIE DARTED FROM THE HOUSE, and into some shrubs. Marlene opened the door and retrieved the empty bowl. Moxie settled into the dry rubbish under the bush.

During the night, he challenged any cat that dared come over the fence. Some he fought and repulsed, and others fled when he charged. It was a popular place. The door opened again. Soon, the scent of mackerel drew him a few steps out of his concealment, but he managed to keep the stray cat's philosophy, and waited until everything was safe. A few minutes later, Marlene got into her car and drove off to continue her daily search for Starlight. Moxie quickly went towards the bowl. Moxie's luck had changed. He bit into the fish cakes and savored the taste. Loud purrs came from his husky throat.

Moxie wondered what this place was. After a moment of contemplation he decided it wasn't important. The real matter was establishing his dominance over this new turf, and with every meal he became fit for that task.

Dark storm clouds gathered in mid-afternoon. If it rained all evening, it would mean a disastrous night of hunting. Seldom Seen rested under a bush for a catnap with Cloudy at his side. He thought of Wisecat. Her words weighed heavily on him and Seldom Seen hadn't seen her in a week. Guilt stabbed at him

Cloudy groomed her coat while Seldom Seen looked at her with half-closed eyes, the tip of his tail flicking back and forth. He remembered Wisecat saying King Rat had to die. He pushed the words aside and focused on Cloudy again. Her grooming finished, she met his gaze with a loving one of her own.

Seldom Seen dozed. Cloudy rose and had a few tuning stretches as thunder rolled in the distance. She saw a flash of lightening too. Cloudy moved on to investigate other sounds, planning to be back before Seldom Seen knew she was gone.

Cloudy hopped a fence with one lithe bound. A strange scent Cloudy couldn't identify caught her attention, but then she heard the noise that drew her out from hiding. Five meters away, birds chirped and cleaned themselves in a birdbath.

Cloudy watched carefully. Some were on the ground eating seeds, while others splashed above. Cloudy crept forward. Snaring a creature that could fly was a great challenge, and one she wouldn't deny herself. Cloudy accepted the invitation with a stealthy tread and sharp wit. She got within a few meters and still the birds hadn't noticed her.

Cloudy paused, every muscle poised, her eyes and brain ready to send her body-bolting forward. She calculated the distance, and the effort it would take to catch one of those birds.

A sleeping dog woke with the feeling that something was in his territory. Glazed eyes opened, and focused on the cat, which was intent on a cardinal on the ground.

Suddenly, the cat lunged and the birds took flight, but one wasn't quick enough; the cardinal. Cloudy snatched it in midair and brought it down. The dog ran headlong into the fracas. In an instant, the hunter became the hunted. Cloudy saw the beast. Overzealous in his attack, the canine overran Cloudy as she fled for the fence. They tumbled in the grass, rolling end over end, throwing up dirt and roots as they came to a halt. The dog's jaws snapped out at her, but she was very quick. She leaped over the fence, and to safety.

It was over as fast as it had started. Cloudy looked at the dog from the other side of the chain-link fence. She would always remember his kind. He snapped and bit at her viciously, his fangs locking on the fence links mixing frothing salvia with his bloody gums. He hated Cloudy, wanting to kill her.

As long as the fence was between them, Cloudy knew she was safe. She cantered away, victorious.

Seldom Seen woke from his doze and found a dead cardinal lying before him. Cloudy purred with pride.

"It's my gift to you! I'm happier than I've ever been. I'm grateful for your help in smoothing my path into freedom, and I love you with everything that I am!"

Seldom Seen sat up, nosed the bird, and then licked it. It was a fresh kill. Seldom Seen devoured it quickly and then he went to Cloudy and licked her head and chest.

Seldom Seen knew, it had been confirmed with this act. His wildest dream took root and became reality. Cloudy loved him.

As the thunderstorm poured its deluge, Seldom Seen and Cloudy relaxed under a bush to keep dry. As gusting winds dispersed the red feathers on the ground, Cloudy purred, telling him about her previous lifestyle. He listened and concentrated on the meanderings of her previous lifestyle.

"I'm great!" Cloudy said matter-of-factly.

"No one has ever beaten me." Cloudy recited her lineage of champions and talked of the future ones she bore who would certainly rise to the same fame as she.

Seldom Seen thought about the things Cloudy told him, and then he realized she'd given all that up on a whimsical chance. A chance to be with him, and that made him feel grand.

Where Seldom Seen came from and what offspring he left behind was lost with time, and circumstances. He realized these facts were what made him so different from her. Cloudy was a pedigree, and bred for the aesthetic pleasures of the humans, where he was naturally fabricated for the realities of nature but still, that very fact is what started their beautiful relationship.

"Have you any offspring?" Cloudy asked.

Seldom Seen gazed at her.

"Tink has recently birthed my seed, but they were destroyed by a rat while newborn, any adolescent black you see is of my seed. I am the Duke of the second quadrant, and no other tomcat has the right to make offspring on my turf."

Seldom Seen painfully told her about that terrible night, in fact it was the very night they met. It seemed like a million years ago, but the tragedy locked the door on his relationship with Tink. Tink had deserted the newborns to find the good aroma that was in the air. Tink never relinquished her old habits, not even for the kittens. It was a hard lesson for them, and Seldom Seen now realized that he was also partly to blame. He had been idling with Starlight instead of hunting that night. That extra time spent with Starlight could've just as well been the cause of the newborn deaths.

"After the fight with King Rat, I went to where Tink and I hid our offspring, only to realize that it was my new litter he butchered. That's when I became familiar with death, and much sorrow. Tink and I have been separate ever since that time, each of us wanting to forget what happened that night." He looked at Cloudy trying to detect jealousy.

Cloudy realized she'd never been in touch with death on such a personal level. "What does it feel like to lose those so close to you?"

Seldom Seen thought for a moment before replying. "In this world, death is the true master. You can't run or hide from it. Don't think about it, Cloudy. It'll come to you in its own time."

MOXIE PURRED TO HIMSELF, PROUD of the fact that he stepped back into a rich lifestyle. Rummaging in garbage cans, and hunting mice weren't his style. He always managed a life of comfort. The last episode at the restaurant was only one of the many leisurely ways of living he procured for his opulent lifestyle. Moxie now had another.

Moxie maintained his domination of Marlene's chow bowl. Other cats learned to stay away from Moxie's new turf or face his bloodthirsty wrath. Those who challenged Moxie fell before him like grass to a lawnmower. After a few more days to master the timing of the meals, Moxie planned to resume his search for Cloudy with much strength and vitality.

The terrible scab finally fell off Moxie's nose, and it made a bulbous shape, and one more tattoo in the catalog of his young, and violent lifestyle.

As the rain fell, Moxie thought of Cloudy. Dreams of Cloudy filled his sleep leaving thoughts of her to haunt Moxie while awake. Moxie barely knew her, but Cloudy's beauty impressed Moxie so much that he wanted her to share his new lifestyle, more than that, Moxie wanted Cloudy to birth his colorful markings with a new litter to show his dominance on the streets. Seldom Seen stole Cloudy, and Moxie knew they were together. Moxie vowed to crush this new enemy and make Seldom Seen feel the full weight of his vengeance, and take back what was rightfully his.

Tink

Tink crept into the dump well past dusk. Cloudy was right, if she applied herself then there was no reason why she couldn't catch mice too. Tink was determined to get a rodent tonight.

Tink's bells tinkled intermittently in the death-like silence. That strongly contradicted with what Cloudy said earlier about nocturnal noises that would help mask the sound of her bells.

The summer storm passed after pouring its torrents upon the land, and cleansing away the dirt and grime of the past weeks. In the dump, the effect was minimal. Periodically, a flash of lightening, and a crack of thunder reached Tink as the storm moved into the distance. She hopped over a puddle. She saw two mice in the middle of an argument.

Runrun, and Alsoran found a tasty hunk of food. They were inseparable; their tails were glued together by a long ago accident. While looking for trash to eat, Runrun dipped his tail into a discarded gallon can of industrial strength glue. They became connected.

Both mice grew accustomed to their sorry predicament. Runrun was the larger and made the decisions. Alsoran was about half of Runrun's weight, and when nibbles were found all situations went in the larger mouse's favor. Other than that, they compromised each other when they had to make progress.

Except for foraging, bickering was the norm, but this time was exceptional. They fought over the possession of a whole sugar doughnut. It was so large not even both of them together could completely eat it, but they fought over the possession of who would get the first bite, paying no heed that the argument was ridiculous.

Tink saw her opportunity, but hesitation made her wonder if she could actually catch a mouse. Tink thought of Cloudy. The Persian's speech gave her the strength to make the attack. Tink acted as if the bells didn't exist.

"I saw it first!" Alsoran squeaked.

Runrun looked at his forced companion. Runrun came close to gnawing off Alsoran's tail in order to rid himself of the headache. Alsoran hopped boldly onto the doughnut. "This time, it's all mine!"

With a heave of his body Runrun toppled the smaller mouse, staring at him with venomous black, beady eyes.

Alsoran tried to keep Runrun from getting the first bite.

The tiny mouse dug into the dirt, and pulled the larger mouse, hoping to drag his opponent from getting the first bite, and then a cat's paw pinned him to the ground. He was missing a large part of his beautiful long tail when Tink separated them with a sharp bite.

Alsoran heard the bells, and then watched his one-time companion disappear down Tink's throat. Tink released Alsoran. He never thought about running away. Alsoran knew he'd die too. Tink hit him hard with a swift paw strike.

Alsoran woke a few minutes later with a bruised head. The sound of bells quickly brought him round. Alsoran knew it was the sound of death. He peered about and saw Tink poised a few inches away. Alsoran wondered why he was still alive. Dull pain came from the end of his tail, and then he remembered that the cat bit a part of it off.

The prisoner fascinated Tink. Such were the pests who had mocked her hunting abilities. After feeding for so long on the tidbits of the humans, eating raw mouse was very distasteful and she didn't want to repeat it. Tink was content in knowing she could catch them.

Tink pawed at Alsoran to entertain herself. Alsoran dare not flee because that might warrant immediate termination. He decided to risk the posture that kept him alive thus far, docility.

He didn't know what to make of the strange cat. Finally, he risked speaking. The tension between them had to be defused, or it would shatter the thin veil that kept him alive. Tink would just as easily kill him, and leave him for someone else to eat.

"You've had your meal. Do you mind if I eat mine in peace?" It was a bold ploy, but ever since finding the doughnut he'd been making brave moves.

Tink eyed the doughnut, and then smacked it within the mouse's reach. Shocked, Alsoran began to nibble on it. Alsoran ignored the cat's presence; if this was to be his last meal, then he preferred to eat it without worrying about what was to come. At least he'd die on a full belly.

Alsoran looked up with powdered sugar on his whiskers, and snout. He'd taken two chances this evening, and both paid off. His only penalty was a missing tail and a bruised head, but he was still alive. Alsoran asked the question that bothered him. "Bell Ringer, why have you spared me?"

Tink stared at the distant lightning flashes in the clouds. "It's because I'm lonely."

Alsoran perked up. Everyone knew loneliness at some point in their lives. Alsoran surmised that Tink's loneliness must be immense. He went to Tink, closer than any sane mouse would dare, and grabbed her by the whiskers, and kissed her on the nose. Alsoran found the cat's weakness, and then lied to save himself.

"I know something about loneliness. In fact, I feared it so much that I glued my tail to another mouse so I'd never have to confront it again."

Tink eyed him. Rodents were some of the most prolific mammals on earth. Cats hunted them because they were so abundant. It was hard to believe a mouse could be lonely with so much garbage around, and mice to eat it.

"Since you took my friend, I'll have to face loneliness again." He pretended despair.

"You're a liar! From what I overheard, you weren't friends at all! I think I did you a favor. Do you think I devoured the other mouse without bias towards you?"

Alsoran's eyes lit with confidence. "I'm grateful to you Bell Ringer for your generosity, but the facts are evident. You owe me!" Alsoran cleaned his whiskers.

Tink watched him. Alsoran was up to something. Perhaps it was time to end the conversation. Tink flexed her claws menacingly.

Alsoran gathered his faltering courage. She smelled like an alley cat; one that rummages through the human waste as he, and his kind; plus no other reason could possibly substantiate her presence in the dump.

"We need each other Bell Ringer. I can show you the best places to get human trash. I'm a mouse, and I know such things. I can show you the world! All I want in return is a friend to keep away my loneliness, and I have chosen you!"

Raindrops fell, one final assault from the clouds before they disbanded for a brighter day. Tink left the dump. It was an eventful night, and Tink was proud of herself. She'd seek out Cloudy and thank her for the advice but first; she wanted to spend time foraging for cheap bites with her newfound buddy. Alsoran clung to Tink's collar, and thought where to go and fill her big belly.

King Rat surfaced from a gutter in Taverny. He was soaked by the torrents from the storm. The sewer system was his avenue to the suburbs. King Rat renewed his search for Seldom Seen.

Along the way while traveling underground he saw broken mice, dead with necks and backs cracked from traps. Others were bloated by poisoned bait. One day King Rat vowed such things would cease. There would come a time when rodents would dominate the earth.

King Rat slunk along the curb; suddenly a terrific pain assailed his hollow eye socket making him stop. He rolled and thrashed on the wet pavement. He cursed Seldom Seen once more. The pain was one thing that kept the cat firmly in his mind, and it supplied the fuel for his drive for revenge. He was a super rat, yet an ordinary stray cat had maimed him.

King Rat recovered in a few minutes, but he noted that such attacks happened more frequently. The diseased eye socket was slowly taking hold of his health. Sometimes, he felt as if a dagger was being wedged into his brain. After fathering his new breed he didn't fear death like before though. If King Rat died then it just meant he wouldn't be around to witness the Age of the Rat. He was like a God to the other rodents, and that sufficed his ego.

The genetic engineers knew their business; he was the largest of fifteen super rats. King Rat wondered if the other genetically altered rats truly realized their worth as he did. King Rat remembered the lectures he gave them in the pitch-blackness of the sterile lab. Most of the time they slept through his long-winded speeches, but that never stopped him. The act of speaking brought him avalanches of new thought. Sometimes the other rats managed to mock and tease him into silence, but still he never let his dreams die.

King Rat watched as an opossum hurried across the glistening street. He beckoned it, and realized there was nothing more ugly than a wet opossum. "Do you know me?"

The opossum rose onto her hindquarters to let her babies see from inside the marsupial pouch. The tiny faces popped out one after another. "Yes, I've seen you on top of the Palace in the city dump. You're the Long Talker."

"Then tell me where I can find the cat I seek!" Hatred swelled in King Rat's heart upon thoughts of his archenemy.

The opossum shook her head and retreated before the rat's vengeance was unleashed on her. Every denizen of the night knew of the unfinished business between Seldom Seen and King Rat. King Rat often raved against all cats while in the confines of the dump. He'd conquer cats first because they were the spoiled playthings of the humans. If rats were to rise beyond their present status, then the felines must be dealt with first.

Cats were the sworn enemies of all rodents, and Seldom Seen was the worst of all for he tried to kill King Rat. There was never enough slander heaped on Seldom Seen. When the time came, his suffering would be outstanding. King Rat often got his mob in an uproar, but he made them wait for the deciding factor that would ensure victory.

King Rat wondered which way to go. He'd gone near and far seeking Seldom Seen during the past weeks. Someday they'd meet, but the anticipation of revenge was poisoning his ultimate goals.

An hour later he was in front of the old cat he killed weeks ago. Wisecat was foolish sending an assassin against him; that merely ensured her death. He thought of Wisecat's plan and the attack by Seldom Seen; it put paranoia into his mind. It couldn't have been a coincidence. These two cats had been after him from the start of his escape. They knew King Rat's destiny was real and they tried to thwart it, but he was stronger. The carcass before him proved it. The aged female would spin no more plots against his budding empire.

The horde of rodents had devoured Wisecat and her bones and fur held feasting maggots in the remaining putrid flesh. Wisecat's dismembered head sat upright a few feet away, almost defiant against her end, the sunken eyes now alive with the movement from the feast within. Nothing about the carnage revealed the once brilliant mind that was her trademark.

King Rat would wait here as usual for Seldom Seen to return. The cat had to come back if all what Tutulem said was true. King Rat sat quietly in a darkened corner of the attic, relishing the moment when he'd witness Seldom Seen's agony over the death of a dear friend. At Seldom Seen's weakest moment King Rat would seize the opportunity to kill him. The closed quarters of the attic would give him a better advantage than the wide-open spaces where they had first fought.

King Rat conjured horrible fantasies about Seldom Seen's death as he waited. The fantasy endeared most was gnawing right through Seldom Seen's neck until his head fell off, that torture would surely be a slow and painful death.

King Rat went to the attic portal. Seldom Seen had vanished. King Rat had been waiting in ambush every night for weeks without the slightest sign that the cat had come back.

The glow of the rising Sun caught his attention and he didn't want to be caught outside in the daylight. King Rat headed back towards the Palace, for the moment the night was his only domain. King Rat scurried off in the dawn. So far, his efforts for revenge were fruitless.

THE SOUNDS OF CIVILIZATION SUCCUMBED to nature's pleasant enchantment. In the distance, leaves on the trees sparkled with a million points of reflected sunlight from the breezes. Seldom Seen's gaze spanned the mountain-like hill he and Cloudy were on top of.

Below, a great expanse of summer flowers splashed the slope with brilliant colors, and it would be Seldom Seen's and Cloudy's playground today.

They ran headlong down the slope and into the field of flowers. Cloudy led the way, darting and feinting in the dense growth trying to elude her pursuer, but Seldom Seen wouldn't give her up.

Colors and fragrances streaked by in an endless procession that blurred her senses. Fresh and flavored scents energized her with a feeling that she was a part of what was happening in nature, and Cloudy enjoyed the feelings of being totally unrestricted. It was wonderful to be chased, to be wanted and to be free.

Seldom Seen lunged for Cloudy and brought her down in a stretch of mature dandelions. A cloud of fluffy seeds blasted the breezes, traveling to fulfill their destinies. Mocking paw strikes cuffed his head and sides repelling his attack, and then she righted, and darted off, leaving a trail of dandelion seeds aloft in her wake.

Seldom Seen gave chase, but she immediately vanished. He paused because the game became more interesting now. Seldom Seen eased through the grass and flowers, trying to see her movements. His sight pierced through the flowers. Bees buzzed angrily around his head seeking to sting him because of the ruckus, but he slapped away the persistent ones.

Cloudy couldn't be far-gone, and emotionally Seldom Seen felt she was very close. It wasn't a game of chase, but hide-and-seek now.

Cloudy crouched low as she saw Seldom Seen move in her direction. The flowers were so thick he'd never see her in the cloud-like, dandelion fluffy seeds. She was the prey, and intended to be a very difficult catch. Cloudy's heart pounded with enthusiasm and her spirit soared with the stratospheric clouds.

Seldom Seen saw a flash zipping through the dandelions, and forced his lithe muscles into long strides and leaps, giving chase like no other cat could. Cloudy's tail flashed in front of his eyes and blinded him as she sprinted to escape.

Cloudy didn't escape. She gave one last effort to delay the end, but Seldom Seen brought her down an instant later.

They tumbled headlong into a heath of blueberries. Cloudy didn't fight back, but embraced him. Seldom Seen turned her over and gave tender bites and licks, feeling refreshed and alive because of the capture. Seldom Seen was drunk on love, as long as he lived he would love Cloudy.

Cloudy was a passion stronger than anything he'd ever known and Seldom Seen would always surrender to it without question or pause. Juice from the crushed blueberries stained her coat, but Cloudy didn't care because she was in his embrace again.

The odor of the rotting berries on the ground gave a pleasant, but intoxicating smell for the two felines. Seldom Seen watched Cloudy as she went through the laborious task of removing the burrs from her long coat. Her genetics weren't made for nature's measures. A pattern of berry stains tattooed her back and flanks. A few minutes of play led to all this disarray, but even as a mess her beauty showed through, it was something that welled up from deep within Cloudy, never to be dulled by outside forces. This was her essence, an inner strength to explore and adapt to anything that was new. It took some coaxing but it was always there, and she responded once tested. Cloudy's physical beauty was the first intoxicant for him, but Seldom Seen was drawn to her by more than that now.

Tink groomed herself carefully. It was the mid-afternoon chore to keep her orange tiger markings clean and presentable after a long morning of can hopping for bites. Alsoran showed Tink a few of his better spots for dining, and she had a belly full of good chow. Their budding relationship was going smoothly; perhaps both were ill from the specter of cat-versus-rodent. They risked something new and bold in a world that didn't accept change. Alsoran promised to meet her again in the dump at dusk.

Finished grooming, Tink cantered off towards Seldom Seen's turf. She'd definitely find Cloudy there, and then she'd be able to boast of her accomplishments like Cloudy did.

Around the neighborhoods, three strong tomcats held a bit of turf they called their own. As always, the strength and wits of the Duke reflected the boundaries. In such a hierarchy, only three tomcats held territories, or Dukedoms, and holding a territory made them Dukes being privileged to sire offspring.

They were in descending order, Moxie, Seldom Seen, and Bossy. They had earned the right to sire offspring. The remaining tomcats were too young, old, or weak to maintain the virility level necessary to be competitors, and those tomcats roamed from one Duke's turf to another's until chased away.

Moxie was the youngest by a good measure, but he held the largest domain of all the Dukes, and a majority of the kittens born the last season held his distinctive tri-colored markings, but as Tink moved through Moxie's turf she sensed it was abandoned. Moxie's male scent was very stale. A young tomcat poked through the hedges.

Tink recognized him. He was inexperienced, but because of his hunger to be the best he was ready to cross the line, and take a territory of his own. He'd been defeated a dozen times by Moxie, but T-Rex always returned for another chance to topple the king-pin and take over. Moxie's disappearance left him with a golden opportunity now. Moxie had punished T-Rex severely every time he challenged, but the young cat's path was finally clear.

T-Rex was ready to pay with blood, or his life in order to win his own turf. True defeat was assured only when one quit. Tink paused, unsure of T-Rex's attitude. His tail went bushy with preliminary fear, and then he relaxed after identifying the female, who was no threat. T-Rex went about the business of marking Moxie's old turf with his new scent.

"YOUNG FOOL!" Tink meowed.

"Better ones than you have tried to take what Moxie conquered. What makes you any stronger or wiser?" Tink moved closer to hear his reply.

"Moxie is no more." T-Rex's young eyes met her eyes with assuredness.

"He's vanished. I'm just one of many who are splitting up his turf."

That was big news! Moxie had to be dead; there was no other way this could happen. There would be noisy nights of fighting as other tomcats arrived to fight over this opened up turf.

T-Rex was a handsome tomcat with areas of black covering his eyes like a mask and moving down the front of his snout marking him with a large T. Other areas of black broke the white along his back, and cascaded down the right side of his hind leg. His tail was solid white with orange markings on both forelegs. Green feline eyes gave his face the appearance of a possessed demon with lively color.

T-Rex showed scratches from many bouts. He was sore, but a winner and satisfied with the outcome of the previous night's fighting, which he had won. It was just the beginning though, other tomcats would arrive to unseat him, but until then he was a Duke, any female who came into estrus on this newly won turf he had rights to. With this big step T-Rex won the right to sire offspring, and start his own tradition with kittens that would pass on his camouflage markings.

Nervous energy filled Tink as she realized the old order was rapidly changing. Moxie had been supreme, an accomplished master of the streets, and a legend even at the tender age of four years; it usually took four years of strong determination to carve out a Dukedom. Moxie's sudden disappearance without a trace left a vacuum for another tomcat to rise to the top. Hard fought battles would be waged every night.

T-Rex was still very much unproven. Tink assumed he'd fall at some point when stronger and wiser tomcats came to fight, and claim this opened up area, especially Bossy, a seasoned Duke, but now waning due to years, but perhaps this new situation would allow a second rise by the silver gray. Manny's *Dumpster* was the key to superiority in this quadrant. For now, the upstart T-Rex had dethroned his father.

Tink moved on, wondering how Seldom Seen fit into that. Whenever turbulent winds blew, the Black Duke was always involved. Tink sensed Seldom Seen was the cause of Moxie's so-called demise.

Moxie sat on the picket fence and observed his new turf, but it meant nothing. As long Cloudy eluded him the puzzle of his life was incomplete. Moxie needed her to make him whole. The loss of Cloudy preoccupied him.

Moxie never gave a second thought to any female, and only a few hours with Cloudy showed him how cheap life had been. Cloudy gave him a taste of what Moxie really wanted, and he wouldn't let her escape.

In Moxie's life events came and went, sometimes with drastic consequences, but it was different now. Moxie had always been the mover, but now he was the moved.

After a brief grooming, he dropped to the sidewalk. Moxie had already beaten all adversaries and secured his new turf, but it was far from his old territory in the ghetto. The houses and lawns were unfamiliar. There were a few strays he recognized, but the rest were weaklings. These cats didn't have the strength it took to be Dukes, or even hard-core stray cats. Most wore collars showing that their masters let them roam part of the night; being fed regularly dulled the raw instinct of a natural hunter and killer.

Being housed on a regular basis was enough to dull their native aggression, making them easy for Moxie to beat. The domesticated cats couldn't possibly overcome his raw savvy for the streets, and his fighting skills. With his past shattered and his future still unformed, Moxie began his first search for Cloudy since forging his new turf.

Moxie's most severe wound was completely healed, and he was ready to do battle for Cloudy again. Cloudy had double-crossed him, and she wasn't going to get away without his full wrath.

Moxie moved along the sidewalk. Deep inside though, he wanted to bring Cloudy to his new turf and forget the defeat suffered on that evening they first met. Moxie found another paradise and wanted to rule it, and Cloudy. Marlene fed him in the early morning, just before the Sun rose, and in the early evening before the streetlights came on. Moxie felt certain that the next time a meal arrived; he'd have Cloudy back. The hunt for Cloudy's love was on.

Alsoran relaxed in his den, which was packed with straw, cloth and other tidbits to make him comfortable. Alsoran thought of Tink. She devoured Runrun, the mouse who had soured his days and nights with abuse. With proper manipulation he could wipe out all opposition and build a small empire underneath King Rat. He might even be able to challenge King Rat. The possibilities were limitless!

Alsoran sat in his den and molded the plans that would get him from being a nothing player to becoming the ruler of all rodents. If he could develop terror among the denizens of the dump by displaying his power over Tink, then he could rule them.

Alsoran had two possible courses. The first was to form a small underground empire beneath King Rat's own, providing King Rat could actually succeed in his plan to conquer the humans, but how long could such an affair last before earning the super rat's wrath. Perhaps he should try to kill King Rat outright. Alsoran was willing to pit Tink's hunting skills against the super rat's savagery. Destroying King Rat would show everyone how mighty he was. Alsoran liked the second idea more. He'd kill the super rat, and then tutor the offspring to obey him as the high ruler.

Each night the rodents gathered at the Palace to hear King Rat's philosophy, and how he was about to change the world, it would be the perfect time to assassinate King Rat . Alsoran brushed his whiskers with his forepaws, and sentenced the super rat to death. It would have to be dramatic, and witnessed by many. All would know that he managed the super rat's death. Riding on Tink's collar in the moment of truth would give the effect he desired..

Alsoran pictured himself hanging onto Tink's collar like a broncobuster as Tink leaped from the top of the heap to kill King Rat. The bells would tinkle its song of death as they flew through the air.

Alsoran squeaked with glee, but before he could be king he'd have to gain Tink's trust, and food was the means to that end.

THE NUCLEUS OF MOXIE'S PHILOSOPHY is wishing what you want, and then doing the very actions to acquire the goal. Moxie was an opportunist, exploring different situations, and creating others he could exploit. That's how Moxie got to be the best, and he applied those tactics in his search for Cloudy now.

With the Sun high above, Moxie was in familiar territory, the ghetto. Moxie paused at the back door of Manny's kitchen. The broken screen door had been replaced with a brand new shiny one.

Moxie peered through the screen to see Manny and another cook in a refurbished kitchen, and working the lunch hour rush.

Moxie backed away, and hopped onto the *Dumpster* and it was replaced with a larger one, reflecting the increase in the business through new advertisements.

Just recently, Moxie could've strolled through the broken door and into the kitchen, and demand food with a loud meow. Those days were gone! Moxie risked his life just coming back here, but this is where he met Cloudy. Perhaps she'd be foolish to return. Moxie decided to wait, and find out.

This restaurant had contributed greatly to Moxie's rise as the king pin in the ghetto. It gave him that slight edge that all winners take to victory. Moxie was a bit larger than most tomcats, and that difference in weight was because of Manny. His food gave Moxie the energy to overpower any tomcat that challenged him. The restaurant was Moxie's great shield against the worst the streets offered too. In the winter it kept Moxie warm during freezing nights when Manny let him roam the floor to hunt mice in the restaurant. Moxie remembered the days before finding Manny when he crept under one warm car after another to keep warm on a cold winter's night. There were never enough cars to keep him comfortable all night.

The aroma of Manny's cooking came to Moxie's disfigured nose, but he sat patiently and didn't attempt to recapture the old lifestyle with a loud meow. Moxie made a step into the future, and wouldn't try to hold onto the past lifestyle.

Moxie sat on the *Dumpster's* rim and looked into it. The smell of cooked meat reached him. A few maggots crawled up the sides of the bin only to fall back into the trash. That oasis of discarded morsels was once a gourmet dining spot for him, but it was below the new standards he acquired with Marlene's food. There was no sense trying to reclaim this old turf. Fighting for something he couldn't capitalize on wasn't sensible. If he'd kept returning to this old turf, Manny would eventually kill him. He had really damaged that man.

Moxie saw a tomcat in the alleyway poised to attack, probably the new Duke of quadrant one, and the *Dumpster*. Moxie flexed his shoulder blades. He leaped casually to the ground and moved towards the other tomcat. That gesture alone would've sent most cats retreating in flight, but T-Rex's moment of truth had arrived. T-Rex moved towards Moxie ready to defend this prized bit of turf.

Moxie gave the upstart a fleeting glance, and then vanished through the alley before T-Rex could react. Moxie didn't want to waste time and energy fighting for something that would be to his detriment. Cloudy was out there, but she wasn't here.

Seldom Seen and Cloudy pushed through the thick bush. His thirst was strong and he hungered too. They shifted from a playful tone to one of nourishment and survival. Their playful attitudes reinforced the feelings that they were only for each other. They were one, never to be separated.

Seldom Seen entered a wonderful lifestyle. It was almost unreal to think it was happening to him, but the grass, ground and the sky made it real. Cloudy was with him, and would be so as long as she would have him.

Cloudy broke into a leisurely stride, releasing some of the energy that yearned to be spent. Seldom Seen followed passively. Cloudy wasn't trying to get away now; she only wanted to hasten the next episode in their lives. Cloudy paused and caught his gleaming yellow eyes. "Teach me all there is to know Seldom Seen."

Cloudy felt weak in the open after living so long in a house. She was determined to catch up and set her life on the path to absolute freedom. The Black Duke was her answer. Seldom Seen promised to do that and more. She'd never know it but he wanted Cloudy to be more than what he'd first found.

Tink moved on. The neighborhood was changing with dizzying speed. Seldom Seen had been swept away by a newcomer. As long as she knew him, he'd been approachable, but suddenly he was a stranger. Tink looked for him, but he had vanished into the embrace of another's love. Tink remembered the days when she could summon his love.

HOT SUMMER DAYS ARE TAILOR-MADE FOR LOVE. Seldom Seen and Tink relaxed under the shade of a willow tree and took in the soft breezes and summer sounds. These were the long days when the Sun rose early and set late. Tink leaned against the Black Duke. They were lazy with love. Tink purred softly against his chest, glad he was her champion.

They'd met one morning while looking for bites. The tomcat took a liking to Tink and took her on as a partner. They fell into a companionship of fun and love building a bond to last. He'd have Tink when no other would consider her as a running mate, fearing her bells as a bad omen.

Unfortunately the death of their newborns signaled the end of their passionate union. Tink would never recapture his flame, but with things as they were, Tink hoped he was still well. Seldom Seen would always hold a special place in Tink's heart no matter how distant he became.

Tink entered onto Seldom Seen's turf. Tink thought about Moxie, and didn't believe he was dead. Moxie was too smart and indestructible. Tink wondered how Moxie fell from his high position. Tink felt there was a common thread that bound all those events. Time and again her cat sense pointed towards Cloudy. Before Cloudy everything was normal, and then suddenly with her appearance life was amiss, the status quo sent tumbling into a tailspin to destruction.

Tink stopped. Wisecat knew everything! Wisecat would shed light on the events and make sense of all that recently happened. Tink made hasty tracks towards Wisecat's lair, and wondered what she'd say and most of all, what would occur next.

SELDOM SEEN AND CLOUDY WENT about the business of getting a quick meal. It was okay to search through a Duke's turf during daylight. That was peacetime for warring Dukes, but once darkness fell, then getting caught on another cat's turf called for swift retaliation.

Under those dark conditions, Seldom Seen stole Cloudy from Moxie. If Moxie was as proud as he usually was, then that meant he'd be back for another fight someday. Seldom Seen knew Moxie wouldn't rest until he had Cloudy back with him. Moxie was the only thing that might destroy their love.

Seldom Seen led Cloudy to some garbage bags for cheap bites that would sustain them until the evening hunt. He quickly clawed at a bag to get some morsels. Cloudy watched, learning something new. With a little persistence, Seldom Seen extracted a few bites from within the garbage bag. Cloudy pushed her head into the bag and brought out more of the same.

Seldom Seen licked his chops, and then surveyed the surroundings and satisfied himself that no danger lurked. Stray dogs were the worst threat. They were as mobile as cats, and had more rights to the streets than any other animal. Yes, canines were so powerful and deadly that there was no way to reckon with them. They ruled the streets, and they never took prisoners. Any feline fled at the sight of them.

Secondly, but more devastating were the cars. Those behemoths roamed the streets all day and night, in rain and clear weather. Only when they were silent could they be approached safely.

Disease was the only thing a wary cat couldn't fight, and the biggest taker of lives. By the time a cat showed any symptoms after contact with a diseased cat, it was too late.

Seldom Seen warned Cloudy about those dangers often, but she still carried a lackadaisical attitude as if the streets were not dangerous. Cloudy refused to learn the S.P., The Stray's Philosophy. For now, Seldom Seen was Cloudy's guardian angel. He couldn't do it all the time. Eventually, she'd be in situations without his protection, but until then he'd spend extra time looking out for her. Wisecat did it for him, and he in turn did it for Tink.

He couldn't imagine the day when they'd separate. Nothing lasted forever, but Seldom Seen tried to make time stand still as he built a future for himself and Cloudy.

Seldom Seen grabbed a few more morsels and beckoned Cloudy to do the same. It was time to pay Wisecat a long overdue visit.

Cloudy caught Seldom Seen's scent markings as they entered onto his turf again. It was an aroma she smelled during her first days on the streets. If she had only known whose turf it represented back then, now she'd always remember the scent of his markings.

Shadows hid them from the Sun as they moved along hidden pathways known only to cats. Eventually, they reached the mighty oak tree, and passed over the hundreds of acorns rotting on the ground under its branches.

Just overhead, hidden from the weather, and dangerous streets, lived the cat that knew everything. Cloudy looked at the small portal through the leafy branches, seeking the Siamese's image against the dirty window. Cloudy was happy to be able to see Wisecat again. Cloudy would boast to Wisecat that she had accomplished her goal.

They moved onto the rooftop. Blistering heat waves bounced off the black tar of the roof and the streets below. Cloudy's vision spanned the neighborhood yards and streets. Pigeons sat comfortably at the far end of the roof, keeping an eye on the felines. For a second, Seldom Seen was apprehensive about entering the hole in the roof. Seldom Seen remembered Wisecat's words. He decided since King Rat hadn't been active there wasn't any particular urgency to kill the super rat as she had demanded.

Both cats went into the attic carrying food for the aged feline. In a few seconds their eyesight would become accustomed to the dim light. Seldom Seen dropped his offering as he caught the overpowering smell of death. He paused and waited for his keen eyes to tell him what had happened. Too many times he caught that odor when he found a dead cat on the streets. He surmised Wisecat had finally died in her sleep.

Seldom Seen would pay his respects, and then leave and return no more. Cloudy inhaled the odor, and knew it meant death even though it was her first whiff of it. Cloudy ate her offering to Wisecat knowing it was no longer needed.

The starkness of the sunlight from the portal softened to a humble glow as their eyes adjusted to the darkened area. Cloudy saw it first, Wisecat's head sat erect in the middle of the window's light and her body lay beside it.

Seldom Seen felt lightening bolts charge his emotions and he bolted insanely, running up the insides of the roof until gravity pulled him down. Seldom Seen landed in the insulation and he attacked it in frenzy, sending clouds of debris into the air.

Wisecat had been murdered! The dismembered head was King Rat's trademark. Seldom Seen blamed himself for Wisecat's death, and the full weight of his vain actions crushed him down. Seldom Seen edged his way out of the carnage and crept towards his mentor.

Seldom Seen's black form was etched forever into Cloudy's memory as he darkened the light. Cloudy couldn't move upon seeing something she wasn't supposed to ever view in a champion. In a breath, Seldom Seen was a million miles away from her. She'd always felt close to Seldom Seen, but now his naked being lay revealed to Cloudy.

He sat in front of the dismembered head looking into the lifeless eyes for solace without finding any. Seldom Seen's head drooped in sorrow, and he looked into the bloodstains dried on a large spot on the wood planking where Wisecat bled her life away. In the insect infested body, beetles and maggots moved under the decomposing fur giving the illusion of life where none existed. Seldom Seen looked out the attic window thinking of all that Wisecat gave him; and the most prized gift, life.

Seldom Seen trembled like a sick kitten. If only he'd been more in tune to what Wisecat told him, but he fell in love. Seldom Seen's shallow breaths barely filled his lungs, and he was frozen in a death-like trance.

"Why now?" He moved away never wanting to see, or even remember this place and be reminded of how he failed a trusted friend. Seldom Seen turned towards the opening in the roof and saw Tink sitting beside Cloudy. He moved to them with a humble gait. Seldom Seen was totally destroyed.

Both were silent. He caught Tink's gaze, and then Cloudy's too. Seldom Seen's words were firm, but his emotional weakness showed. "Today in this dim and stale place, I lost a part of my life. I beg both of you to never come back here."

They nodded solemnly in unison.

Seldom Seen's voice became strong and vibrant. "Death to King Rat, I will go where he thrives and kill him!"

Moxie

THE SUN BEGAN ITS FAREWELL dive as it passed its zenith, and slowly edged towards the horizon. Moxie eased from his resting place. Moxie wasn't the cat waiting for something to happen. His restless nature constantly moved him towards destiny. The only way to get a hold of Cloudy was through hard work, and relentless action. He was now fit for that very task.

Moxie looked around, and paused to clean his whiskers. Moxie was back in tune with his old surroundings. Somewhere out here was a moment for him to be with Cloudy again.

Moxie moved on, keeping his senses acute. Moxie pawed past opportunities to dine on cheap bites, because he was beyond that level of survival. Like a shadow in the night, he cut through a group of hedges onto a hidden route into Seldom Seen's turf. Moxie never cared about the Black Duke until he stole Cloudy.

Moxie appeared onto the street again. If he found Seldom Seen, then he'd find Cloudy too. He paused in the middle of the street. His broken tail drooped towards the pavement. He looked around wondering which way to go.

On the rooftop the trio finally left Wisecat's tomb, and went to the edge of the roof. Seldom Seen was in shock. Cloudy, and Tink shouldered his sides giving him support. Tink licked the side of Seldom Seen's head offering her condolences, but the black cat was numb to everything physical. Seldom Seen was the traitor; the one who'd turned his back on a just cause when most needed.

Cloudy looked out over the rooftops. The heat waves were reduced as the Sun set. They'd been in the attic a long time to mourn Wisecat. Birds were flying back to their roosting places for the night, a sure signal for hunting. Perhaps a good night of hunting would snap Seldom Seen out of his sad mood.

Cloudy looked at the streets below, and felt a rush of alarm. Moxie was there! Moxie licked his paw, and then moved towards the mighty oak, oblivious to the trio's presence on the rooftop. A cold chill gripped Cloudy. She begged Tink not to move at all. Cloudy didn't want the bells to sound a presence that Moxie wouldn't ignore.

When Cloudy was with Seldom Seen, she managed to keep Moxie from her mind. Now, all her memories of Moxie rushed back with vivid awareness.

Moxie moved towards the mighty oak. Cloudy panicked as her fascinating lifestyle suddenly crashed into ruin. Just when life was magical, and grand she had to deal with the death of Wisecat, and now, Moxie's reappearance. Cloudy now understood the ups, and downs of being a stray.

Tink watched Moxie. He was alive! Tink admired his masculine savvy.

Cloudy told Tink about the battle between Moxie, and Seldom Seen. "He's a brigand, and the worst decision I've ever made. He wants me, a fate I want to escape! Please help me!"

Cloudy added how Moxie hurt her, and she dreaded the thoughts of being with him again. Cloudy became frantic as she begged Tink for help.

"I have to get Seldom Seen away before Moxie finds us! He'll kill Seldom Seen for my treachery!"

Seldom Seen stared into the sunset unaware of their conversation, or the matter of Moxie being on the street below.

Tink moved along the limb that led from the roof.

She looked at Cloudy. Tink was resolute in confirming her plan of action, "I'll lead Moxie away from here. Moxie won't listen to me, if he suspects something is amiss. You must hurry to get Seldom Seen away!"

Tink went down the trunk hind legs first, and then jumped the last few feet to the ground. Tink saw Cloudy through the branches as Moxie approached her.

Tink thought to herself, "You owe me babe."

Cloudy meowed thanks as Tink went to block Moxie's advance.

Tink went straight towards Moxie without hesitation as his tail went bushy with preliminary alarm.

This was the first time she got a close look at him. Moxie's lifestyle was legendary, so young, yet very accomplished. Tink looked at Moxie in admiration. He was very strong. His battle-scarred frame was full of hidden muscles. Moxie seemed invincible.

The tension eased when Moxie saw that Tink was no threat. He sized Tink up for worthiness. He slapped at the bells. "What curse is this?"

Secretly, Tink was drawn to his rough magnetism, but she was determined never to let him know. His macho charm veiled the true nature of his cruel personality.

"It's no curse."

Tink flicked her tail. "I'm so good at hunting that I had to figure a way to make it harder."

Moxie gripped into the oak for the ascent. Tink drew his attention with a mellow purr, "Don't you find me attractive?"

She did a stretch to emphasize her form.

Moxie looked at Tink, and then thought of Cloudy. "You're nothing! Move along before I give you some misery!"

Tink backed away, retreating from the oak; and his threat. Moxie went up the oak trunk, and disappeared into the leafy branches.

Tink meowed, and loud enough for him to still hear, "Perhaps you'd find my friend more attractive. She, you can't resist I know this. Cloudy's a strange one, but the most beautiful pussy you'll ever see!"

Moxie rebounded from the tree, his heart pounding. Moxie was in front of Tink. His meow was firm, and direct. "Take me to Cloudy!"

Tink groomed her forepaw. "Cloudy has no time for a hooligan like you! She's courting Seldom Seen's love."

Moxie's claws unsheathed at the mention of the Black Duke.

Tink continued, "Do you know him?"

Moxie looked at Tink, raw jealousy in his eyes.

Tink continued, "Yes you do! Let's see if you're savvy enough to win her, for brute strength alone won't ensure your victory."

Tink sauntered away from the tree to a new destination.

Moxie followed Tink's lead.

Cloudy watched them from the rooftop. A heavy weight settled on Cloudy as she took the lead in caring for Seldom Seen. She waited an extra minute to make sure Moxie, and Tink were gone.

Cloudy loved Tink, and she'd always remember the unselfish deed. During that minute, Cloudy tried to understand the turmoil Tink must constantly feel, knowing another female had Seldom Seen's love.

Cloudy would try to survive the night, and perhaps in the morning, Seldom Seen would be back to normal. Cloudy quickly went down the tree, and moved in the opposite direction. Seldom Seen followed her. There was no time to feel anything for Wisecat. She would do so later, when danger wasn't prowling so close.

Moxie followed Tink. Meeting Tink was a stroke of luck. Moxie swelled with confidence as he realized the quest was coming to a head. Moxie would crush Seldom Seen, and show Cloudy who was the number one Duke.

Moxie stopped; perhaps things weren't what they appeared. He knew Cloudy was treacherous, and she'd certainly fight him along with Seldom Seen against his victory. Moxie realized he'd have to fight both again, and perhaps Tink too.

Moxie meowed for Tink to stop, but Tink quickened her pace. Moxie couldn't risk losing the chance to get Cloudy now. Moxie prepared to smash all three!

Seldom Seen kept stride with Cloudy's pace, and she moved urgently, but he just wanted to slow down, and sort out what happened to Wisecat. His mentor was gone forever. All the fun cherished with Cloudy that morning went stale in his mind. He was the deserter; the one who abandoned Wisecat's cause, and was led astray by selfish passions. Seldom Seen wished to die, and be punished for what he allowed to happen to the Wisecat. When he looked at Cloudy ahead of him, he realized right then, that his wish was a shallow one.

Twilight faded to darkness. In the highlands near the dump, heavy fog formed. Tink led Moxie into the depths of the home of the rodents. Moxie felt the passing of time with great urgency. Moxie's heart pounded as he thought of seeing Cloudy again. Moxie was ready to explode as Tink stalled, taking him from one place to another, all fruitless, only with the true intent of leading Moxie farther from the sought after duo.

Now, deep within the dump Tink paused for the last time. The surroundings looked like a hell spawned nightmare. Heavy mist floated on the warm stinking breezes. Tink planned to abandon Moxie here, and go about her business with Alsoran. Tink smiled within herself for being so clever.

"I've done everything I could to lead you away from them. Hopefully they're long gone by now."

Moxie looked at her in astonishment. His cat sense finally realized he'd been duped. "You led me wrong, why?"

Tink eyed him with malice. "Cloudy saw you! Yes, you were that close to her."

Moxie turned towards the way they came, but Tink stopped him with a mocking mew. "I know you, I've watched you from afar for a long time, and I've seen the way you demolish lives for the pleasures of yourself. Your style would destroy her beauty. I vow that she'll never be yours to bastardize. Let them live in peace!"

Tink turned her back on Moxie, and moved off to keep her appointment with Alsoran.

Moxie was deathly silent. Moxie watched her go, his whiskers fanning from his face in rage. His orange eyes lit with the flames of revenge. Tink made a fool of him!

Seldom Seen relaxed, and watched the midnight. Cloudy went off to hunt for both of them. He began the painful task of putting himself back together. Above and to the right, he looked at a bright star. It stood out like a bright pinpoint. The star shined its distant light on him with the wisdom that love was unstoppable; it always found a way to manifest. Love came at any time, and place with a multiplicity of matches from far and wide, to high and low. Seldom Seen was wise enough to grasp the opportunity when it arose, and he reserved the right to love; it wasn't selfish passions that drove him to be with Cloudy, but true love.

Seldom Seen realized he couldn't blame himself for what happened to Wisecat. The only tragedy was that it happened as he fell in love with Cloudy. Wisecat was a firm believer that events happened exactly at the times, and under the circumstances prescribed by nature. All events were staged with perfect timing, and design, and nothing was an accident, but part of a grand design. Wisecat foresaw his love affair with the newcomer, and the unnatural problem of King Rat who was created by Man.

Wisecat's death was a fact, and she had accepted it without a qualm. Wisecat threw her last stick of fuel onto the flames of Seldom Seen's heart. Her death reinforced his emotions tenfold. He couldn't ignore Wisecat's words any longer! Seldom Seen had to find King Rat, and kill him.

Moxie thought briefly about what Tink said, and then attacked her. Tink's bells rang as she fell under his strength. Tink fought back desperately unaware until now, Moxie's obsession over Cloudy. Tink couldn't run because the bells would betray her. Tink had to hold her own until Moxie got over his rage.

In the distance, Alsoran heard bells ringing. That meant Tink was keeping her appointment as promised. Perhaps his scheme actually had a chance to succeed. Alsoran decided to take Tink on a round of gathering some even more tasty tidbits than the previous night. Later, he'd spring his master plan on Tink, and convince her to participate.

Moxie slammed powerful paw strikes against Tink's head. Her bells rang with each devastating shot. Tink was dizzy from the barrage, but she resisted Moxie. Moxie bullied his way into her like a battering ram, knocking her off balance, and down; dagger fangs sank into her throat. Moxie had her! Tink pawed the ground trying to stand, but failed. Moxie's jaws crushed her windpipe cutting off breath.

Tink struggled, but she was beaten! Tink's eyes widened with fear, and she convulsed to breathe. Her claws sliced Moxie's shoulders and head drawing blood, but Moxie was in a fighting trance, and felt no pain.

Tink lost consciousness as death took her away. In her last seconds, Tink realized what she'd got herself into with the predicament between Cloudy, and Moxie. Tink hoped her ploy would make a difference in their lives.

Moxie held her up in his jaws for a minute, and then let Tink's lifeless body drop into the trash. Moxie purred with satisfaction; his fit of rage over.

Cloudy returned with a mallard duck. Seldom Seen sat up alertly. He took it from her, and devoured it, feasting on its vitamin, and mineral rich liver, and breast muscles.

Seldom Seen stretched, and announced his mourning was over. He couldn't bring Wisecat back. The incident cast a feeling of seriousness over their relationship. The fun and games that went with love would never be quite the same.

Moxie started the trek back to his new turf. However close he'd been on the trail, it was certainly cold now. Tink was the only stray he ever killed, something inside of him popped.

Tink's treachery had been a rare defeat for Moxie, and her punishment was a quick death. It was getting very serious for him.

Moxie pushed through the fog, and went down the hill towards the meal from Marlene. Moxie would resume his hunt for Cloudy with a full belly.

By the time Alsoran found Tink, the dump's inhabitants were eating her, at least twelve rats, and as many mice ripped, and pulled at the fresh carcass in a feeding frenzy.

Alsoran saw his hopes, and dreams disappear down the throats of those he wished to rule. Alsoran moved among them, and found Tink's body still warm from life lost.

Alsoran gnawed at the weathered collar. He'd planned to free Tink from the noisemaker after they made a solid bond. Alsoran did it now as a farewell gesture to a dead relationship.

Powerless again, Alsoran let his grand visions fall away into failure without trying to restructure them. The episode with him, and Tink sparked a brief flame that lasted a few seconds before dying out. Alsoran fell in with his brethren, and relinquished the illusionary plans spun the previous night.

Seldom Seen, and Cloudy moved through the mounds of trash in the dump. Not knowing which way to turn, he led a happenstance expedition of revenge hoping to find some clue that would lead him to King Rat.

The thick fog gave the night an eerie feeling. It covered everything. The dump was a familiar place for Seldom Seen, even though it gradually changed with the addition and removal of garbage through time. Some things would always remain; the stench, the hordes of flies, and of course the rodents.

This was all new for Cloudy, and her curiosity quickly abated once they were deep within the misty graveyard of doom. She remained close to Seldom Seen as they traced a hesitant path through the hulking hills. It all looked the same to Cloudy. Each corner they turned simply reminded her of the previous sights. As far as Cloudy could see, it was a depressing landscape of waste with endless tons of human trash.

A bat knifed through the thick mist. Its screech echoed like a laugh mocking Seldom Seen and Cloudy. Perhaps they'd never see trees and green grass again, or hear the melody of songbirds and smell the sweet scents of flowers on a summer's breeze. The heavy mist collected in Cloudy's long coat making it hang as if reflecting the toll her spirit suffered from such an ominous place.

Seldom Seen stopped; a furry hulk caught his eye. It lay in bold relief against the rest of the trash. Just ahead was the broken body of a cat, one of the many alley cats who lost their lives while foraging for food in the dump. Usually they were old and beaten down from a hard life on the streets; no longer agile enough to hunt mice.

They moved closer for a better look. It was Tink, ripped and torn to shreds! Hundreds of bites gave testimony of a violent end. The eyeballs were eaten from her skull, and would never again reveal the bright attitude Tink tried to maintain during her unfortunate lifestyle. Tink met a tragic end, and then gutted by feasting rodents. Her days on the streets had come to an abrupt finale.

Cloudy looked at Seldom Seen. Nothing about the situation could bring them any luck. She wanted to leave. The sight of Tink's maimed body would heavily tarnish her memories of the alley cat. Only in death would Tink find solace.

Seldom Seen also read the sign of Tink's savaged body as a warning for any who dared trespass into the rodent's domain. His courage wilted. The sharp edge of vengeance dulled as he pondered the reality of life over death. There was a strong possibility that he, and Cloudy would die in the dump tonight like Tink. Trying to slay a super rat on his turf with an army of rats to fight with him seemed impossible. Seldom Seen felt a desperate need to get away, and take Cloudy from this nightmare.

Seldom Seen looked upward into the fog, it was changing, a portion of the gray mist was glowing with odd luminance. A vision of Wisecat appeared. Wisecat's shape wavered, and was transparent, but she maintained a constant point of focus in the mist. Cloudy peered at Seldom Seen, and then at the point where he was focusing his senses; but she didn't see anything.

"Strong one, we meet again, or could we ever truly part? Not even in death." Wisecat looked down at the torn body of Tink. Another vision slowly materialized; it was Tink!

Seldom Seen was broken. A heavy weight settled on his being. The ghosts looked down at him.

Wisecat spoke, *"This is what will befall all of us if you don't act with courage, and strength. My death and Tink's have started the beginning in a new trend, which must stop tonight! Don't weep for us. We were the sacrifice, the unforgivable crimes that would bring your wrath upon those who want to destroy Man.*

"On this side, I've discovered that your present life with Cloudy is perfect love. Are you willing to forfeit your love for Cloudy to ensure a safe path for those who will live after our time?

More visions materialized in the fog. Like a motion picture, an unseen future played out for Seldom Seen.

It was a desperate time. Poison bait and traps had failed. Cats were nowhere, and super rats roamed openly through the streets sweeping away a bitter history. It was a time of plague and death. As the pandemic spread, men deserted their homes. Clouds of poison gas were sprayed from crop dusters into the forbidden zones, snuffing out every type of life except the super rats. With every gas attack, the rats went underground. Sewers had saved their species for thousands of years and did so again. Birds, dogs and cats died as the ill winds spread out making them unwanted causalities, but the effort to kill the disease carrying rats continued without success.

Deep within himself, Seldom Seen felt something growing stronger every second and it hammered his heart to smash the bond between himself and Cloudy, his emotional being staggered along the edge of sanity.

Tink spoke, *"Now isn't the time to let your love for Cloudy act stronger than logic! You must do what must be done! To falter now is to die as we have. Humans have created a new breed of rat. You must destroy that which would rob freedom and joy for us all. Above all else,* **YOU MUST KILL KING RAT AND HIS SPAWN!"**

The apparitions swirled away into the fog as Tink's last words echoed in his mind. Seldom Seen climbed to the top of a nearby hill of trash, and stared into the distant fog. He was an ebony statue against a backdrop of gray mist, an assassin cloaked in black. Seldom Seen scanned the dump, somewhere out there lurked a dangerous adversary.

Seldom Seen wondered if it was a mistake to bring Cloudy on this mission of death, and destruction. He looked down at her; Cloudy was his strength, and his desire. No, it was no mistake. Cloudy belonged with him. Seldom Seen unsheathed his claws, and flexed them repeatedly. The fog was thick, but he saw clearly what to do.

Flashbacks of the last few weeks with Cloudy drifted lazily through his mind. Seldom Seen allowed himself a few moments of happiness before setting out on the grim task from which he couldn't hide. Before Cloudy could follow he vanished into the heavy fog, and was gone!

CLOUDY WONDERED WHAT JUST HAPPENED. She gazed from the top of the hill of trash where Seldom Seen had just been, and a bat broke the silence as it fluttered pass with a shrill laugh. Uneasiness gripped her threatening to become terror. Abandoned, Cloudy moved in the direction she thought Seldom Seen went.

Alsoran poked his head out of Tink's hollow carcass. Alsoran thought he was dead for sure when the two cats came upon the carcass, so eager to feast that he ignored the stampede of fleeing rodents with the proximity of the cats getting nearer, but his luck held out.

He'd gain great favor with King Rat with the news that his archenemy was roaming the dump. Alsoran might even become a coordinator in the super rat's spy legion. Everyone knew that King Rat's spies received the best of everything. Alsoran decided to be one, and with this valuable information he could name his price. Alsoran went towards the Palace in great hast to tell King Rat that Seldom Seen was back in the dump to kill him.

Seldom Seen halted, and glanced around. He didn't see Cloudy anywhere; while concentrating to kill King Rat he didn't realize she was left behind. He backtracked until he found the spot where their paths most likely parted.

Cloudy was gone! Once again the fabric of his very being became torn. King Rat would have to wait. Seldom Seen's priority quickly changed to not leaving Cloudy alone in this hell-like place.

Cloudy roamed aimlessly. Movement gave her a sense of security, sitting and waiting was too nerve-wracking in this place. The dump was a place for the dying and she wondered why Seldom Seen brought her here. Cloudy moved on, seeking some evidence of him. She heard rustling under the trash as mice fled her approach.

Alsoran entered the throne chamber. King Rat lay asleep. It was too early for him to make his nocturnal rounds. Spread out in the shredded trash of the chamber was bundles of baby rats. Some were white, while others were spotted with gray, but all were abnormally large. Alsoran moved among the princes, and princesses, giving homage to those he disturbed from their quiet sleep.

All the female rats were away feeding and King Rat was left to guard his genetic brood. Once they returned then he'd be free for the rest of the night.

King Rat squeaked with glee at the news Alsoran brought to him. He'd finally get his revenge! A long-awaited debt would be collected tonight. King Rat scurried off to find Seldom Seen.

The next evening he'd announce to the masses that Alsoran was his new spymaster. King Rat scurried out into the foggy night. If the information was fresh, Seldom Seen couldn't have gone far from the freshly killed alley cat.

Cloudy gave up after a fruitless search for Seldom Seen in this wasteland. She cursed Seldom Seen for being a fool to leave her alone, but then she wondered if he might already be dead. Cloudy needed to escape from here. Cloudy wanted to be free of the dump with, or without Seldom Seen.

Seldom Seen looked around and couldn't believe he lost Cloudy again. Dire urgency pressed him into relentless action. Seldom Seen became frantic, wandering in circles looking for Cloudy. He wanted to meow but didn't dare because that would bring a horde of rats against him. He was the only chance Cloudy had of leaving the dump alive. It was a monumental task, but Seldom Seen refused to give up until she was safely in his presence.

Cloudy found the Palace; it rested in the fog like a strong fortress. It seemed like a stroke of luck. Cloudy remembered home, and how that always meant safety with its enclosure. She circled the car, and then leaped inside through the broken door.

She investigated the large compartment. The seats were ripped and mildewed, but she had really lost the taste for pristine surroundings. It would be a sufficient place in which to sleep away the rest of the night. Cloudy surmised she'd be safe here, and in the morning find the way out of this maze with daylight on her side.

Cloudy settled down to sleep, and thought of the characters she met since the escape from Tavenry. Tink's help, and deed would always remain priceless ones. Tink was the first feline from the other side to lend Cloudy some advice, and help her find Seldom Seen. Taking another female to someone with whom she'd had an affair was something Cloudy wouldn't have done; her motives were always based on herself. After dealing with Tink, she'd make it a point to be more humble to others. Cloudy knew Moxie had something to do with Tink's death.

Cloudy wondered how Wisecat was so strong. She was thankful to have crossed paths with the Siamese, and learn the proud history of felines. The way her death touched Seldom Seen, and the pain he felt touched Cloudy too. Seeing him wither away in seconds was almost too much to bare. Cloudy's love for Seldom Seen would always be strong. Seldom Seen filled her life with life.

Moxie; as long as Cloudy lived on the streets there would be tomcats like him to force their will on her. She puffed with anger about the scars he inflicted on her stomach, and wished he'd die, and then the suffering of many would cease.

Cloudy finally realized that this lifestyle wasn't hers, nor could she make it so. Cloudy was an oddity on the streets. She'd soon succumb and be destroyed by the brutal forces that pressed from all sides. Cloudy was bred as a purebred domestic, and it was time to find a way home, a way back to Marlene.

Noise caught her attention from the rear of the car. It was the familiar squeaks of mice. Cloudy realized she was hungry. Earlier, she hunted for Seldom Seen and not herself. She crept to the rear and saw a passageway into the trunk. Hesitantly, she stuck a paw into the darkened hole, but felt nothing. More squeaks beckoned her to enter into the deep dark.

Cloudy found King Rat's litter lying there. They were blind and helpless without their protector. Some squeaked for milk sensing her presence. Cloudy went to work on the newborns, eating some, and killing the rest outright. She felt no mercy for them for now it was natural instinct for her to kill vile rodents.

King Rat circled the vicinity where Tink was killed. He was cautious, not wanting to alert Seldom Seen to his presence. After a brief preliminary search it was evident that the cat was gone. Then he realized his grand blunder! His offspring were unprotected with cats roaming the dump! King Rat scurried back to the Palace.

Seldom Seen paused in the night, and twisted his head trying to hear words that weren't quite audible. Like a whisper Wisecat's voice came to him. *"I love you."*

An apparition of the Siamese appeared before him. Wisecat was translucent and bathed in a golden aura. Wisecat looked at him, *"I'll lead you to Cloudy. She's in trouble!"*

Wisecat ran off.

Wisecat rushed through the fog without disturbing it. Seldom Seen followed. Wisecat ran through obstacles over which Seldom Seen had to vault over. He threw all his reserves into the chase fearing to lose sight of his guardian angel.

King Rat approached the Palace. All seemed tranquil. He crawled into the rear seats and the scent of an alien intruder came strongly to him. His worst fear immediately crystallized; there was a cat in his sacred domain! King Rat charged into the opening that went into the trunk ready to deal death to the intruder.

Cloudy turned around to see King Rat when a flash of lightening illuminated the chamber with an eerie flash. King Rat saw her too in that same instant with one of his dead babies hanging from her jaws; blood smeared down her chest.

Wisecat led Seldom Seen a long way in a short span of time. As the fog parted, he finally saw King Rat's Palace. Seldom Seen's chest heaved, and he tried to catch his breath as he bolted after Wisecat's ghost down through the passageway and into King Rat's throne room.

Wisecat's image flashed into lightening as she crossed the threshold and straight into King Rat pinpointing the super rat as a target. King Rat leaped for Cloudy's throat. For a split second King Rat was illuminated in midair. Seldom Seen made a desperate lunge, and caught the super rat in midair knocking him into a dark corner. The fight was on!

The flash left Cloudy blinded, but she heard a terrific struggle between King Rat and Seldom Seen. Although short on breath, Seldom Seen attacked the rat with mass fury. His paws cut like razors, slicing the rat's hide, and spilling blood. King Rat bullied him into a corner, and there they tangled in a blast furnace of hatred.

King Rat's tail thrashed like a bullwhip, and he squeaked with rage, all his babies were killed. He'd take both their heads off for this sacrilege. All the time and effort spent to start his dreams were smashed by Cloudy.

It was pitch black in the chamber and Cloudy's mind almost shattered as she listened to the battle, and wondered what was happening. Seldom Seen gave a mighty hiss, and then came heavy thuds as his paws struck home. She heard a brief scramble in the trash; and then all was very still.

Seldom Seen took in heavily loaded breaths. He'd been bitten on the left side and in his hind leg. King Rat bled from several superficial scratches, and fang punctures. King Rat thought of escaping, but he paid a high price to get a chance to kill the black cat. He'd slay Seldom Seen and Cloudy, and then start over with more babies.

Seldom Seen's vision slowly grew accustomed to the darkened trunk. There, directly across from Cloudy was the super rat. King Rat couldn't see the black cat but he easily saw the Persian crouched in a corner. Seldom Seen saw her too, so far she was untouched.

King Rat lunged for Cloudy and Seldom Seen attacked. He crashed into King Rat with brutal finality that neither might survive. They were locked in a death grasp.

Cloudy listened as terror numbed her from action. She dare not join the fight. Cloudy never saw a rat that large and it frightened her. She heard both struggle in one another's grip, and then came silence. King Rat bit deep into Seldom Seen's neck. Seldom Seen grimaced in pain, and blood spurted into the super rat's mouth. King Rat meant to have Seldom Seen's head right now!

Seldom Seen did not wither away from the death match, but locked his jaws onto King Rat's windpipe shutting off his air. Neither could break the death grip, or tried. The furious battle of a few seconds earlier stopped as both settled down to see which one would live.

Cloudy couldn't see what was happening in the dark, but she heard Seldom Seen's rasping struggle to breathe. At least he was still alive. She also heard the ravenous gnawing of the super rat, and that sound left her pale with horror. Something dreadful was happening.

Cloudy didn't want Seldom Seen to die, but she was frozen to aid him.

King Rat was choking. He had no breath, and the cat's blood really began to pour into his throat. His pink eye rolled upward in dizziness, but his chisel teeth never stopped cutting through Seldom Seen's neck. He shredded through fur and muscle and finally struck a big artery.

Seldom Seen's grip grew weaker every second. He knew the giant rat wouldn't quit until his head fell off. Seldom Seen felt the pain that made him want to break his bite, and run away but he bit harder. He had to kill King Rat and fulfill Wisecat's wishes even if he must die.

Seldom Seen became faint, and relaxed with the flow and the dreamy state that beckoned him away. He didn't resist. Seldom Seen's consciousness went away and calmness came to him. The warmth and pleasant sounds that drew him away from agony came from a summer meadow. It was good to be gone from the death match.

Seldom Seen was at the edge of a pond, and it was a bright sunny day with silent breezes bringing various scents to his nostrils. Lush growth in many colors abounded everywhere. Clouds slowly drifted past thousands of feet above, very untouchable.

Seldom Seen looked about and was content. Gossamer butterflies danced on the wind seeking nectar. He groomed a paw, and saw the soft golden aura radiating from his body. It didn't alarm him though, and seemed natural to glow. He knelt to quench his thirst because fighting made one thirsty. The cool water tasted good. As he looked up from the water's edge, Wisecat was there. She was across the pond, strong and healthy, a young feline again. He was awestruck!

Wisecat gazed at him with clear eyes. Suddenly, Seldom Seen realized he was dead and in the afterlife. The fight was over and he had been killed. Soon Cloudy would be at his side too! King Rat would make sure of that, and then he and Cloudy could live happily in this paradise. He had failed Wisecat again; and now Cloudy.

Seldom Seen battled anew and fought to get back into the hellish agony that he willingly left. He couldn't die, not now! Above, the clouds accelerated as he focused his thoughts on Cloudy. Seldom Seen refused to perish from an earthly life as long as love for her existed in his heart.

The scenery slowly revolved with him at the very center. With each revolution, Wisecat moved in a little closer to him. She sat quietly, and then her form floated onto the surface of the pond without sinking into the water. Faster, and faster the background whirled. Only Wisecat remained in focus. Everything else became a blur of color and sky.

Finally, the two cats met. Seldom Seen peered deeply into Wisecat's big eyes, those beautiful clear feline eyes. Wisecat licked his forehead, and purred a final farewell. Seldom Seen sank into the ground as if slipping into a pool of water. Wisecat stood on top of the ground, and looked down at the vortex as Seldom Seen slipped through the dimension he entered.

Excruciating pain, and the stench of trash assaulted him. He was alive! Not even in death had he released the super rat. King Rat was limp in his mouth. The test was over, and Seldom Seen won the macho test. King Rat was dead.

In severe pain he meowed for Cloudy's help. Cloudy went to him. Cloudy couldn't see him, but her instincts sensed that something awful had happened to Seldom Seen.

KING RAT'S CARCASS TURNED COLD in the waste of his dead babies in the throne room. Cloudy and Seldom Seen together smashed his goals! The cause of King Rat's end was simple; a hunger for vengeance against Seldom Seen secured his own downfall. In the dump the Palace would be a reminder to those who savor mad dreams.

Cloudy hastily led Seldom Seen from King Rat's tomb. In the hazy night his wounds were clear. Rich blood oozed from the side of his neck at a steady rate. His suffering was great.

Seldom Seen felt the remainder of his strength ebb away as he left a trail of fresh blood on the ground. Seldom Seen was dying, but he desperately wanted to be away from the dump. There was a very strong threat of being discovered and attacked by other rats. His last efforts were to lead Cloudy from there and to safety.

It was an agonizing journey, and Seldom Seen crumbled to the ground several times, only to rise on stoic determination to make it to the suburbs. His goal was to take Cloudy back to Marlene, and then die alone. In that way Seldom Seen could spend his last hours in peace. He would be freed of worry about the dangers Cloudy couldn't handle alone; above everything he couldn't tolerate the idea of her with another Duke.

Cloudy followed, at first with sorrow for his suffering, and then with pride at each stealthy tread of his paws. Cloudy realized what a bold and courageous tomcat she was with. Seldom Seen was as much a champion in his world as she'd been in her upper-crust world, but in actuality Cloudy would never have to sacrifice her life, or suffer as he was now. Seldom Seen offered his life for her without hesitation.

Cloudy relived how he bolted through the passageway with a flash of lightening, saving her when she expected a gruesome death. Cloudy realized how shallow her victories at the shows were compared to the life, and the situations on these savage streets. Yes, she had the look, and genetics of a champion, but Seldom Seen embodied the true essence of a champion.

They finally reached the picket fence from which she sprang. On the other side a never-ending food supply.

Seldom Seen sat on the sidewalk. "This is your true home, your best lifestyle. Go back to it because this is where you belong."

Seldom Seen with painful effort leaped onto the barrier to make her follow. The fence brought back a memory, and he thought of the happier circumstances in which they'd met. Here he had snuffed out a mouse's life, and soon Seldom Seen would release his own life. As same with the mouse, he had no way of changing his end.

Cloudy leaped, and then sat on the narrow edge of the fence and faced him. Cloudy saw her home and the doorway where their relationship began. She came full circle. Cloudy was none the worst for a bit of adventure, but her influence in Seldom Seen's life had been devastating! He was dying. Perhaps if she hadn't summoned Seldom Seen that evening he'd be healthy now. Cloudy wondered how many other lives she unknowingly fractured or torn asunder during her brief time on the streets.

Seldom Seen meowed, "Never let me die in your heart, there, I'll always be alive."

He had to appear strong during their last moments together. Seldom Seen wanted her memories of him to be strong and positive ones. Seldom Seen leaped to the sidewalk and painfully looked up for one final glimpse of Cloudy.

Cloudy seemed unreal, a fantasy he had embraced. Seldom Seen caught her gaze with a flash of emotion. Cloudy was the most beautiful feline he ever met, but her physical looks were only the thin veil that projected what lived deep within her being. He had caressed Cloudy's life with the warmth of his love revealing her true beauty. Cloudy had the resolve to face life on any level, beyond, or beneath her station. Other pedigrees would've crumbled under the pressures she just went through. The ability to adapt, and the courage to try something new was her true beauty.

Cloudy was worthy of any feline, but Seldom Seen managed to be the only one in her life. In the beginning, he was swept up by Cloudy's persona and naiveté. Now he wouldn't have her anymore. After tonight he'd never touch or see Cloudy again.

Cloudy looked down on him and purred, "I love you Seldom Seen. Please don't leave me!"

Seldom Seen blinked his eyes several times to clear his double vision. He wouldn't damn himself for giving all he had, a life. Seldom Seen gazed upon Cloudy. Cloudy loved him, and with everything that was within her being.

Death had pressed against Seldom Seen all evening, and now it was making its final approach seeking to snatch him away.

Seldom Seen felt the urgent need to sleep, a slumber he'd never wake from. Blood pumped from his ghastly wound, and his satiny black coat was caked with it, dripping down the front of his furry chest.

Seldom Seen looked at the sidewalk, and saw blood splash on the concrete like teardrops shed over broken dreams. Seldom Seen wobbled, and then crumbled to the ground almost out of consciousness. His muscles twitched trying to hold onto a portion of life. He didn't feel the excruciating pain anymore; only a dull throbbing reminded him of his fatal injury.

Dreamy visions passed through his mind of Cloudy and his previous lives. She was the apex of his unsavory lifestyle. He thought of the names he'd known her by, Starlight; the dim radiance of a heavenly body, so massive and powerful that it can be seen from millions of light years away. If one could get close enough to the power and glory of a Sun it would be awesome. Seldom Seen had been blinded and remade by her love.

Seldom Seen knew her best as Cloudy, a high-flying mist of various shapes and densities, sometimes forming thunderstorms. He'd been struck by Cloudy's lightening.

The love affair was over for him and Cloudy. He would let go of life right there being too weak to move on. In the morning he'd be swept away with the rest of the garbage that lined the streets for removal, just another stray cat that met the fate all strays gripped in the end.

Above on the fence the hiss and confusion of a catfight brought him back from over the edge of death. With glazed eyes he saw Moxie!

Cloudy battled Moxie with a hiss, and a swipe of her stiletto-tipped claws and Moxie planned to punish her severely for resisting him. A lightening paw strike sent her sprawling to the concrete. Moxie saw Seldom Seen down there! The Black Duke seemed to be in a very bad way. Moxie leaped to the ground to kill him.

Seldom Seen rose and Moxie ripped into him with unchecked violence. All the days and nights Moxie suffered, all he lost became a ball of concentrated hatred that exploded on the Seldom Seen like a bomb.

Seldom Seen fought sparsely. He retreated to the street to escape Moxie's vicious assault. Finally all three clashed under the naked light of the street lamp. Cloudy rose to the battle and fought valiantly for Seldom Seen's life, vowing not to let him perish under Moxie's revenge. Every time Moxie attacked Seldom Seen, she unleashed a barrage of paw strikes from his rear. Flashing fangs, and a spirit that refused the inevitable pitted her courage against the most ruthless adversary she'd ever challenged.

Moxie spun around unleashing dangerous paw swipes that cut her chest and face, but Cloudy stood her ground. Cloudy no longer feared Moxie, not caring anymore to receive physical damage while trying to save Seldom Seen.

Moxie managed to lash the dying tomcat with precision though. His paw strikes caught the shredded flesh of Seldom Seen's hideous neck wound. Moxie wanted to pull Seldom Seen in to deliver a choking bite. Moxie wanted to suffocate Seldom Seen, and redeem the defeat by him. Killing Seldom Seen and taking Cloudy back would achieve that end. Every time Moxie managed to hook the black cat, a fusillade of paw swipes reminded him of the nose injury inflicted a few weeks ago by this nimble black cat.

In the still of the night the cats hissed and battled. A bedroom light came on in the house, quickly followed by the opening of a window shade.

Seldom Seen's remaining blood splashed the street. For the moment he and Cloudy managed to keep Moxie between them in a stalemate. Moxie couldn't turn his back on Cloudy, and Seldom Seen still had enough fight in him to keep Moxie from outright killing him.

Moxie swelled with rage over Cloudy's continued betrayal and he channeled it on Seldom Seen, a salvo of strikes sent the black cat to the pavement. Cloudy went to his rescue but another outburst knocked her to the ground too! Moxie paused; Seldom Seen didn't get up.

Moxie's moment had finally arrived. Here was the tomcat that stole his future, and Seldom Seen was beaten! If they fought a hundred times Moxie knew he'd win every one.

He watched Seldom Seen rise on trembling legs. Moxie turned towards the beautiful longhaired Persian. Moxie meowed with confidence, "I'll kill him and then the love and devotion you foolishly bestow will also die!"

Cloudy's eyes sparked with new hatred. Seldom Seen slumped halfway to the ground again, the exhaustion too great to allow him to remain standing.

In the moments that Moxie tested his relationship with Cloudy, Seldom Seen desperately tried to pull himself together. He unwittingly delivered Cloudy straight into Moxie's new turf. Seldom Seen had to keep fighting to save her from Moxie's misery.

Moxie realized that brute force, and threats wouldn't sway Cloudy to his side. She'd rather die fighting his advances and he didn't want that. Moxie longed for the warmth of her soft body close to his as it had once been.

Moxie gave a meow, "He's beaten! Why do you resist me?"

"YOU ARROGANT FOOL! NEVER WILL YOU HAVE ME AGAIN, NEVER!"

Cloudy continued to scold Moxie with sophisticated rage.

For the first time in all of his lives Moxie felt weak. Moxie wanted to strike her down but couldn't. Instead, he tried to bargain for her loyalty.

"I have changed! I do love you, and more than that, I was with you first!"

"YOUR STUPID RULES MEAN NOTHING TO ME! I"LL NEVER BE YOURS AGAIN!" Cloudy struck his face with a paw swipe that cut Moxie.

He didn't retaliate.

Moxie looked away from her and glanced at the Seldom Seen. Considering Seldom Seen's health he'd be dead in a few hours no matter what happened with his effort to take Cloudy back by force.

"I'll spare his life just come back to me."

For the first time in his life, Moxie offered mercy. Moxie would've never thought of it if Cloudy hadn't turned on him. Moxie realized that brute force couldn't win her. Moxie continued to persuade her, ignoring Seldom Seen with all the callousness that the victor shows to the vanquished. Moxie painted a lifestyle she had only experienced with Seldom Seen's love.

That made Cloudy think of Seldom Seen and the times they spent together, the sunny days and the long nights in search of adventure and bites, and how the peaceful purring of his masculinity sent chills through her. Cloudy loved Seldom Seen so much.

She had to accept Moxie's offer if Seldom Seen was to have any chance at all to live. Otherwise, he'd be killed right now. Cloudy's heart was breaking. Cloudy realized that she'd never see Seldom Seen again. There would be no more love between them.

Seldom Seen watched, and listened as Moxie came closer to taking his most precious treasure. Cloudy stared at Seldom Seen, she was willing to do anything to save him, even become Moxie's toy. Cloudy looked into Moxie's eyes and sacrificed herself to his oppressive lifestyle with a solemn nod in order to save Seldom Seen from death.

At that very moment she realized what love is, it's the surrender of your wants, the subjugation of your needs for another's happiness, or in this instance, Seldom Seen's life. This is her lesson learned for becoming Cloudy.

Moxie gazed deeply into her eyes trying to penetrate her emotional defenses, but he failed. No matter, at least Cloudy was back with him. Yes, when the traumatic events cleared things always went Moxie's way. Moxie smiled his famous smile, the one when victory was assured.

Seldom Seen reached deep into his heart and gathered what was left. He got up again! Phantom energy pulsed through him. Seldom Seen pounced on the unsuspecting calico with new vigor, punishing Moxie with blazing paw strikes!

Moxie was caught off-guard and Cloudy was frozen in disbelief. Moxie went down under Seldom Seen's sudden attack.

A speeding car squealed around the corner almost losing control as it sideswiped several cars and accelerated towards the fighting tomcats. Cloudy saw the twin lights and dashed under a parked car for safety.

Seldom Seen ripped into Moxie with total commitment to kill him. It would be his final battle, and would end this war between himself and Moxie over Cloudy.

Moxie saw the car coming but couldn't get away from Seldom Seen's buzz saw attack. The teens accelerated upon seeing targets to hit.

Marlene ran out the front door. Marlene's heart pounded in her chest. She saw Starlight from the window.

Marlene screamed.

One moment the hiss and whine of fighting tomcats boomed like thunder in the misty night, now all was silent except for the roar of the speeding car as it went away.

The fight came to its unpredicted end.

On bare feet, her gown flowing behind, Marlene ran into the street. She saw that the two stray cats were down. Cloudy edged out from under the parked car, and her spirit was at its lowest tide. Marlene picked her up and examined the Persian for injuries. Except for a few scratches she was fine. Marlene went to the tomcats.

Moxie was ruined. He fell directly under the tires of the car. and no life survived in his flattened form. Cloudy looked briefly at him. Her wish came true, and Moxie would dominate no more, but Seldom Seen lay only inches from him deathly still. Marlene recognized him as the black cat that beckoned her doorstep one early morning.

Starlight escaped from Marlene's embrace to go to him. Starlight circled the body several times trying to see life, but finding no sign of it. Tonight she lost everything; even some of her life force went away with Seldom Seen.

She sat in front of Seldom Seen to mourn his passing. She thought of Wisecat and Tink too. Everyone she met while on the streets was now dead.

Marlene knelt, and lifted Starlight from the destruction of Seldom Seen. She patted the Persian gently, grateful that it hadn't been her prized cat that was hit by the car. She looked at the black cat, and planned to give him a king's burial. He probably was the one who brought Starlight home. Seldom Seen had fulfilled the wish Marlene asked of him.

With Starlight in her arms Marlene knelt and rubbed his head in a final farewell. Seldom Seen's tail twitched! There was still a spark of life in him! Marlene examined him carefully for broken bones, and crushed organs but found none.

Besides the wound in his neck all Seldom Seen had was a swelling knot on his head when the bumper of the car nicked him. Yes, death had swarmed all over Seldom Seen tonight, but the black cat had been lucky. He was still alive.

Epilogue

STARLIGHT POKED HER HEAD OUT of one of the circles in the traveling pet case. Her suspicions were confirmed, another cat show. It was a large extravaganza, but to her it would be just another boring day.

Seldom Seen poked his head out of another case. Marlene had saved his life, and Seldom Seen was none the worst for all of his hard fought battles. Around his neck hung a loose-fitting black leather collar made of soft eel skin that hid King Rat's devilish scar to him.

It wasn't intended to restrain him, just accent the beauty of a cat. It was encrusted with real diamonds, rubies, emeralds, and sapphires. In the small loop hanging underneath was a license.

Starlight showed so much affection for the wounded tomcat that Marlene couldn't put him to sleep. After getting him treated by a veterinarian, she took the black cat in and dubbed him Othello after a great Moor warrior depicted by Shakespeare. Seldom Seen's new lifestyle would be a great one and the best ever.

Othello looked at all the magnificent felines sitting in their stalls, each attended by a human. He was stupefied, and wondered if the world had turned upside down. Not in his wildest dreams could he envision such a lifestyle. He looked on as several pedigrees were brushed and prepped for judging as Marlene walked to her designated stall.

Every breed abounded, Abyssinians, Siamese, Burmese and Manxes. He saw Japanese bobtails, Persians, Russian blues, and Angoras, but none surpassed Starlight's elegance. All had exquisite manners and grooming, all were far above his meager beginnings.

Both Othello and Starlight's heads bobbed as Marlene walked to

105

her stall to prepare Starlight for competition. Marlene was filled with excitement! With the coming of the national championship her long-lost energy resurfaced. True, she had missed the last one with the disappearance of Starlight, but now Marlene was ready to recapture the title with her dethroned champion.

It felt good to be back in the middle of the action again. Marlene lifted both cats from the traveling cases and placed them in Starlight's stall.

Starlight and Othello got along fine. If they weren't cat napping or entwined in each other's embrace, then they were engaged in mischief and exploration, the grand old house was big enough for that.

Red carpet runners cushioned the pathways for the judges and admirers who'd come to inspect each cat's genetic purity and grooming. Streamers of assorted colors hung from the huge room's rafters. Before each stall, a cluster of perfumed flowers accented each cat's station.

People talked and traded speculations and it added the final touch for the elite owners who would scrutinize, and then praise a grand champion.

Marlene was the center of this attention. Owners wondered if her Persian could reclaim her spot or forever sink into history as one the best that couldn't rise to the lofty level again.

Othello looked around and knew he didn't belong here. He was just an ordinary stray cat. The others here were kings and queens with royal lineages going back many years.

Starlight had the opportunity to regain her title, but it meant nothing to her. What mattered was the presence of her personal champion, and the time they shared together. In her own unerring way Starlight convinced Marlene to take him in after he healed instead of setting him back onto the streets. The black cat would never have to worry about another meal, or face the realities that haunted stray cats.

You know, there wasn't anything to live for out there on the streets anymore. Starlight gained enough street savvy to perform in her moment of truth when she destroyed the super rats, and that experience would last for the remainder of her sheltered life. From this time forward their lives seemed blessed.

Othello looked out into his new world as Marlene groomed Starlight. He was regal as he sat at attention and took in everything. His coat shined with the black silkiness of grooming and vitamins. The jeweled collar set off his presence like a newly crowned king.

He remembered the dark vicious night where his life had ended for a few moments. Othello probably would never completely realize just what he, and Starlight accomplished that foggy evening in the dump, but when he woke from the nightmare wrapped in her warmth a grander reward couldn't have been given.

He knew both sides of the equation now. He reveled in a new world, but he'd always remember the old one. For a few moments he fancied himself as a pedigree. He couldn't imagine how any cat could walk away from such a luxuriant lifestyle and roam the streets as Starlight had done.

He suddenly realized Starlight staring at him. The sweet scents of jasmine and hyacinth reached his nostrils as he gazed into that familiar look in her eyes. Starlight was in love with him. She licked his ear a few times; it was Starlight's favorite place to lavish affection on him. She gave a satisfied purr.

Othello reflected on his situation, and surrendered to it with a broad smile. With all the hoopla, and pedigrees about he finally realized that this place was exactly where he belonged, at her side.

Printed in the United States
by Baker & Taylor Publisher Services